SHADOW
of the
BUTTE

Thomas Thompson

G·K·Hall&Co?

Boston, Massachusetts
1993

Also published in Large Print
from G.K. Hall by Thomas Thompson:

Outlaw Valley
King of Abilene
Forbidden Valley
Bitter Water

TO MY AGENT, JOSEPH T. SHAW,
WHO HAS BEEN MY BRIDLE AND
MY SPUR.

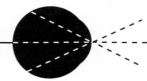

**This Large Print Book carries the
Seal of Approval of N.A.V.H.**

Published in Large Print by arrangement with
Thomas Thompson and Brandt and Brandt Literary Agents, Inc.

G.K. Hall Large Print Book Series.

British Commonwealth rights courtesy
of A.M. Heath Agency.

Printed on acid free paper in The United States of America.

Set in 18 pt. Plantin.

Library of Congress Cataloging-in-Publication Data.

Thompson, Thomas, 1913–
    Shadow of the butte / Thomas Thompson.
        p. cm. — (G.K. Hall large print book series)
    ISBN 0-8161-5481-3
    1. Large type books. I. Title.
PS3539.H697S48 1993
813'.54—dc20   92-25176

The man and the woman rode their horses out onto the high plateau of Anchor Ranch. The sun was at their backs, throwing a red light across the expanse of juniper and sage and cured grass. Ahead of them was a rise of ground from where they could get a splendid view of the canyon where the sun built fires in the shallow stretches of the John Day River. The man turned easily in his saddle, a strongly built man in his middle twenties. The sun was bronze on his angular face. "The river is the east boundary of your uncle's ranch, Miss Ellen," he said. "We can ride up on the hill there and take a look at it."

"If you wish, Mr. Donnelly," Ellen Tremaine said. It was her first visit to the West, and the expanse of land frightened her when contrasted with the confines of Philadelphia. She glanced at Hamp Donnelly, and he had pushed back his hat. She saw his hair, the color of the cured grass, his skin the color of the sun on the butte at their backs. It was hard to distinguish between the man and the land itself. The thought worried her. She was spending too much time thinking about Hamp Donnelly. He fascinated her. But only because he was different from anyone she had ever known before, she hastened to assure herself. She reined her horse and followed him up the slope.

They had ridden together all afternoon, talkative and quiet by turns, as strangers are, Hamp Donnelly pointing out the boundaries of the ranch, showing her the landmarks. To him everything about Anchor Ranch seemed vitally important and deadly serious, and his attitude told Ellen that he felt she, too, should feel this importance. She found that attitude slightly irritating, for she had seen it not only in Hamp Donnelly but also in Dusty Tremaine, her uncle. It was as if they considered that she had come here to remain permanently instead of on a one-month vacation which would be over in two more days.

Two more days and she would return to Philadelphia. A month ago she had dreaded the thought of ever returning. Now she welcomed it.

They rode to the top of the rise and reined up. A small breeze came, bringing the scent of the land, cooling her skin. She turned to Hamp Donnelly, intending to say that the view was beautiful, knowing that was what she was expected to say. She was smiling, a pretty girl with fair skin and gray-green eyes and copper hair. The smile froze on her lips and she said nothing. The wicked anger she saw on Hamp Donnelly's face frightened her.

He had changed with the abruptness of Western weather and she thought of this land, peaceful one day with Indian summer, violently bitter with its promise of winter the next. She saw Hamp raise himself in his stirrups, the heels of his callused hands against the pommel, his forearms as rigid as compressed springs under the fabric of his weather-faded shirt. The muscles of his face had tightened and there were hard knots at the butts of his jaws. "Wait here," Hamp said. "I'll be back for you in a while." He reined his pony and started down the slope.

Ellen looked down toward the green sweep of the river valley and she saw the band of sheep spread out there across the river. It meant nothing to her. She looked

3

at Hamp and he was halfway down the steep slope, reining his pony from side to side, riding loosely in the saddle, swinging with his stirrups. She was suddenly nervous, remaining here alone, and at the same time a bit angry at the way Hamp Donnelly had ordered her so curtly. She jerked the reins, forgetting to neck rein the way Hamp had taught her, and her horse rebelled nervously. She headed the animal down the slope, following Hamp Donnelly.

Over the scrape of the horse's hoofs against stone she heard the thin bleating of the sheep, the sharp, patient bark of the dogs. The jerking of the saddle sickened her. A strand of red-gold hair pulled loose from under her broad-brim hat and clung across her eyes. The horse lunged across a narrow gully, nearly unseating her, and then she was down into the river flats. The horse picked a jogging, loose-reined trot toward where Hamp Donnelly had already dismounted. There was a second of silence when the entire band of grazing sheep lifted their heads and stared across the river and she saw the other man with Hamp Donnelly. She pulled her horse to a stop and she heard Hamp's voice, sharp with warning: "Get 'em back away from the river, Orvie."

She looked at the sheepherder and saw that he was a remarkably big man, a bigness with no beauty about it. He had colorless eyes and long sandy hair that hung like rope strands from under his hat. His mouth was slack and wide, his lips loose over yellow teeth, his jaw heavy. His clothes were badly used, a buckskin vest two sizes small, slick with grease. His striped trousers were tucked into knee-length boots. He wore a hickory shirt and a huge black sombrero with a jagged tear in the crown. He looked at Hamp Donnelly and his mouth twisted in a broken grin. "Them sheep are on mine and Tuna's land, Donnelly," the sheepherder said. "There ain't a damn thing you can do about it."

"I said get 'em back away from the river, Orvie," Hamp said. His voice was like a whip.

Ellen Tremaine felt the impending trouble. She saw that Orvie, the sheepherder, wore a gun in a holster. She was completely frightened. "What is it, Mr. Donnelly?" she said, riding closer.

Hamp Donnelly didn't look at her. "I told you to stay up there on the hill, didn't I?" he said.

The sheepherder rolled his head on his

5

thick neck and looked at Ellen Tremaine. For a second he weighed the situation in his mind. "Well, now, ain't this something?" he said. "No wonder you like the cow business, Donnelly. Playin' tourist guide to your boss's niece. A pretty filly, too." He took off his hat and made a deep bow. "Happy to know you, Miss Tremaine. My name's Orvie Stinson. Me and my brother Tuna was gonna call on you, but we ain't had no special invites from your uncle lately."

"Move those sheep, Orvie," Hamp Donnelly said. "Now." Hamp had half turned, and Ellen could see his face, angular and brown, his mouth tight and cruel. She had the feeling that this was the real Hamp Donnelly, a man as savagely swift and direct as the weather.

Orvie Stinson put his hat on and took two steps forward and now he was close to Hamp. His right hand was resting on the butt of his gun. "You go straight to hell, Donnelly," Orvie said. "You been playin' big push around this country long enough. The other side of the river belongs to me and Tuna, and you or Dusty Tremaine or no other damn cowboy is gonna tell us what to do with it. Take your high-tone city gal

6

and get to hell back up the hill before I run you up."

The terrifying suddenness and wickedness of what happened next jarred through Ellen Tremaine and left her weak and sick. She didn't even see Hamp Donnelly move, but she knew his fist had smashed Orvie Stinson's mouth. She saw Orvie stagger back and then she saw his huge fist start waist-high and loop up. She heard it land against the side of Hamp Donnelly's head.

Donnelly fell back with the impact of the blow and Orvie was rushing in, clubbing down with both fists. Hamp straightened suddenly, his arm worked like a piston, and Stinson's head snapped back.

The silence and speed of it made it twice as terrifying. There was no sound from the sheep, no sound from the slow-moving, wide, shallow river. Ellen Tremaine gripped the saddle horn until her hands were alive with pain she didn't feel. Her horse sensed her terror and kept shying and snorting, ears pointed. Ten feet in front of her Ellen watched two men trying to kill each other. Orvie Stinson started to curse with a filthy vileness, and now the two men were down on the ground, rolling over and over.

They rolled down the bank and into the

shallow edge of the stream. The clear water of the river churned into mud and a streamer of red spread out into the current. Hamp Donnelly was on top, slugging wickedly with his right fist, holding Orvie under water with his left hand. Ellen was crying and she couldn't control it. She saw Hamp jerk Orvie Stinson to his feet and hold him up. Orvie was gasping and choking.

They came out of the water, their clothes soaked, their hair hanging in strands, and there was blood on their faces. Ellen saw Hamp push Orvie, saw the big man stagger, and then Orvie was clutching at his belt, reaching for his gun.

Ellen screamed, but Hamp was already on the half-dazed man, rocking his head with blows, forcing him back. Stinson fell hard and Ellen saw Hamp's boot grinding down against the gun hand, twisting and tearing the flesh until the hand opened and the gun was free. She felt she was going to faint and she slid out of the saddle and ran brokenly toward the men, calling Hamp's name.

It was over as suddenly as it had started, and Hamp stood there, the two top buttons of his shirt ripped off, his sleeve torn. There was a trickle of blood at the corner of his mouth and he was breathing heavily. She watched him and saw the cold rage in his eyes. As Orvie got to his knees Hamp reached down and scooped up the gun. He sailed the weapon far out into the river. "All right, Orvie," he said quietly, "push those sheep back to your own water hole and keep 'em there."

Orvie Stinson got to his feet, and for a second the two men stood there toe to toe and Ellen thought it would start again. "I'll see you, Donnelly," Orvie Stinson said.

"You will," Hamp promised. "Every time you get sheep near the river."

Orvie hesitated, his chest rising and falling with his breathing. He had lost his hat and he looked toward the placid river and saw the ripples fanning out from where the gun had sunk. He turned back, and Ellen could see his face, mangled and bloody, the stringy hair hanging in front of his eyes, his lips torn and raw. The animal hatred she saw in Orvie Stinson's eyes sickened her. "I can always get another gun, Donnelly," Orvie Stinson said.

"Let me know when you do," Hamp said.

Hamp turned and walked back toward his horse. Stinson lumbered across the shallow river, splashing and stumbling like some stupid beast, and when one of the sheep dogs came near him he kicked it savagely.

Hamp Donnelly picked up his hat from the ground, straightened it, combed his hair with his fingers, and put the hat on. He looked at Ellen for the first time, and in the swift second in which their eyes met she saw neither anger nor regret. "This was comin', 'Miss Ellen," he said. "I'm sorry you had to see it if it upset you. I told you to stay up on the hill." A quick smile touched his lips, but it was spoiled by the trickle of blood at the corner of his mouth. "We still got plenty of daylight to see that view I was telling you about," he said.

"I want to go back to the house," she said. She fought to control her voice. She didn't want this man to see her emotions. She was sick and disgusted with what she had seen, and the thing she wanted more than anything else was to get away from this country and its emptiness and its naked brutality. She thought of her brother Paul back in Philadelphia, and the trouble Paul had caused her seemed small when compared with the violence she had seen here today. "I just want to get back to the house," she said again.

"Sure, Miss Ellen," Hamp Donnelly said. "I'll take you there."

Behind them they heard Orvie Stinson's shouts mingle with the excited barking of the dogs as the band of sheep started moving away from the river.

The terror was gone from Ellen Tremaine and now there was anger in its place. She looked at Hamp Donnelly and saw the blood on his face and the water-soaked clothing clinging to his body. "Sheep have to drink the same as other animals, don't they?" she said angrily.

"Yes, ma'am," Hamp Donnelly said. "The Stinsons have plenty of water for their sheep without using the river. I wouldn't deny water to no animal."

"But the man said it was his own land there on the other side of the river," she said. "Doesn't a man have a right to do what he pleases on his own land?"

"Look, Miss Ellen," Hamp Donnelly said patiently. "Your uncle Dusty has built up a mighty good cow ranch here in Anchor. Someday he wants you and your brother Paul to own it and run it. It wouldn't be much good to you if it was all sheeped off when you got it."

"I believe my personal family affairs are

of concern only to me and my uncle," she said. She hoped she had put him definitely in his place.

He looked at her steadily, and in time she had to lower her gaze. "Miss Ellen,' he said quietly, "any affair of your uncle Dusty is an affair of mine. It always will be."

She had no answer. They rode side by side, silently, the rest of the way back to the ranch. Hamp Donnelly was only a hired hand, she told herself. It was silly to get upset over his doings. . . . They came to the corral and dismounted. Once more she looked at Hamp Donnelly, her chin tilted. She dropped her reins and started to walk away. "Take care of my horse," she demanded over her shoulder.

"On Anchor," Hamp said, "everybody takes care of his own horse. It would be good practice for you to do it yourself. Sometime you might need to know how." She knew he was busy unsaddling his own mount.

For a moment she thought of walking on to the house, just leaving her animal standing there saddled. She was afraid that if she did Hamp would leave the poor beast standing there all night. She clenched her teeth and turned back. She loosened the cinch and she felt like beating her fists against the animal's ribs. One thing she knew for certain right at this moment. If she and her brother Paul ever did inherit Anchor Ranch, and heaven forbid that they did, she would keep it long enough to fire Hamp Donnelly. Just then she heard his voice, soft and pleasant. "I sure did enjoy ridin' with you today, Miss Ellen."

She looked up and he was standing there, his saddle in his right hand. He picked up her saddle with his left hand and smiled down at her, a tall man with a rugged handsomeness about him, spoiled now by the fast-discoloring bruises on his face. She met his eyes and couldn't look away, and she had the feeling that he could just reach out and hold her and kiss her and there wouldn't be a thing in the world she could do about it and maybe she wouldn't want to anyway. . . . It was a crazy, wild feeling and it frightened her.

"You'll make a real cow hand someday, Miss Ellen," Hamp said. He turned, releasing her gaze. "Don't bother about your horse. I was only joshin'." He walked over and put the two saddles on the corral fence.

Ellen Tremaine hurried toward the house, trying to walk with dignity. She could feel Hamp Donnelly's eyes on her back, and it

13

was almost as if he were looking through her, seeing that small panic he had caused. She walked faster and felt she had never walked so awkwardly. She heard Hamp Donnelly start to whistle a small tune. She knew she had never met such a man.

2

Hamp Donnelly watched Ellen Tremaine go into the house and saw the front door slam behind her. She's spunkier than I figured, he thought to himself. That much of her is Tremaine anyway. He led the two horses into the corral and turned them loose and for a second he stood there watching them roll the sweat out of their hides. After three tries the horse Ellen had been riding rolled completely over. "There's a hundred-dollar horse," a voice behind him said. "How did the rider stack up?"

"Judge," Hamp Donnelly said without turning around, "someday you're gonna sneak up on a man like that and get your head blown off."

"Not when the man's not wearing a gun," Judge Norton said. He was an old man, slight and wiry and dry, the coal of his stubby

14

pipe reflecting against the lower half of his seamed face. He was Dusty Tremaine's closest neighbor and closest friend and legal adviser, a man who was taking time to enjoy the sun and the rest retirement had brought him. Judge Norton looked closely at Hamp Donnelly, affection in his eyes. "Don't tell me she scratched you up like that?"

"Judge," Hamp said, "you know the women never scratch at me."

"When it comes to women," Judge Norton said, "I know nothing." A bachelor, the Judge had been a successful lawyer in The Dalles, and twenty years ago he had counted his money and quit, coming back here to be with the people he knew and liked. He owned a few acres of land on which he let meadow hay raise itself. He knocked the coal from his pipe and his face was serious. "Run into Orvie Stinson again?" he said.

"That's right," Hamp admitted.

"What now?"

"Him and Tuna have got a band of sheep. Where they got 'em I don't know, unless they're Boyd Novis's sheep, and I can't figure that —"

"Were they on Anchor graze?" the Judge said.

Hamp shook his head. "Had 'em right up

15

against the riverbank, though, and with the river low like it is now, you know a little coaxin' would push 'em across onto our grass."

"You can't stop a man from running sheep on his own land, Hamp," Judge Norton said.

"Maybe not legally," Hamp said, "but where Orvie and Tuna Stinson are concerned you can't go according to the law. You know that, Judge."

"I know it all right," Judge Norton said, "and so does Marshal Ned Crockett and everybody else, but that still doesn't change the law." The Judge's face was worried and he jerked his head toward the house. "Did she see it?"

"Yeah," Hamp said, exhaling his breath, "she saw it. I told her to stay upon the hill—"

"How did she take it?" the Judge said.

"Not good," Hamp said. "She wants to argue about everything." Hamp grinned. "She's in there now eatin' poor old Dusty's tail out about me, I reckon."

"Dusty will tell her how it is with the Stinsons," the Judge said.

Hamp shook his head. "I don't know, Judge. That girl and her brother mean an

16

awful lot to Dusty. They're the only kin he's got."

"Well," the Judge said, shrugging, "if he wants to leave Anchor to Ellen and Paul that's his business, but I think he's wrong trying to cover the fact they'll have to fight to keep it. And getting that girl out here on a one-month visit and expecting her to learn the ranching business in that time is a little crazy."

"Dusty knows what he's doing," Hamp said. "He always does." Hamp was standing with his arm along the top rail of the fence, toying with a string on his saddle. The Judge refilled his pipe slowly. "You having supper with us?" Hamp said.

"Yes," the Judge said. "There are some papers Dusty wanted me to go through with him and Ellen." He lit the pipe, drawing deeply, and he kept his head down over the flaming match in his cupped hands an unusually long time. Finally he looked up and spun the match off into the settling darkness. He didn't look at Hamp as he tamped the red coal in his pipe with his thumb. "As long as you've tangled with Orvie again," he said between draws on his pipe, "I think you're a damn fool to ride around without a gun."

"I guess so," Hamp Donnelly said. His hand moved over and turned back the open flap of his right-hand saddlebag. He lifted out a holstered .45 and cartridge belt and, packing it in his hand, he walked over toward the small bunkhouse that stood beyond the corral.

Inside he examined the cuts and bruises on his face in a piece of mirror. Orvie Stinson had marked him up quite a bit. The bunkhouse door opened and Hamp heard the familiar, limping step and knew it was Dusty Tremaine, his boss. He didn't turn to look at Dusty. He heard the Anchor owner sit down on one of the bunks. There was a long silence and then Dusty Tremaine said, "Did you know, Mr. Donnelly, that you are brutal and wicked? That you deliberately pick fights? That you are like some kind of a wild animal?"

"What particular kind of wild animal?" Hamp asked, rolling his tongue against his cheek and peering closer in the mirror.

"Skunk, I think," Dusty said.

"As bad as that, eh?" Hamp said.

"What the hell kind of foreman are you, anyway?" Dusty said. "You're supposed to make the girl like the place, not scare her to death."

18

Hamp turned now and grinned at his boss. Dusty Tremaine was a small man with piercing blue eyes. He had a wealth of snow-white hair and a drooping white mustache. His face was thin and drawn, as if by pain, and his hands were gnarled and knotted with rheumatism. One bowed leg was nearly a half inch shorter than the other, the difference in length making him walk with a twisting roll that was recognizable as far as it could be seen. He was stiff in the way old leather is stiff, and there wasn't an ounce of fat on him. "I'm sorry, Dusty," Hamp Donnelly said.

"About whipping Orvie?"

Hamp shook his head. "No, not about that. About her seeing it. I didn't mean to scare her."

"Tremaines don't scare," Dusty said.

"I reckon things are different in Philadelphia," Hamp said.

"It don't change the fact that she's a Tremaine," Dusty said. He stood up and clapped his foreman on the shoulder. There was mellow affection in the old man's eyes. "I promised her I'd give yuh hell, boy," he said. "Try to look like a whipped dog when you come in to supper, will you?"

"I'll do my best," Hamp said.

Dusty started toward the door and stopped. He turned and leaned there against the doorjamb, and there was worry in the seams of his face. "How many sheep the Stinsons got?" Dusty asked.

"Five hundred at least," Hamp said.

Dusty shook his head. "I hope they don't try to push 'em across that river before Ellen leaves here," he said. "I wouldn't want her to see that."

"I'll see to it they don't, Dusty," Hamp Donnelly said quietly.

For a long moment Dusty Tremaine stood there looking at Hamp Donnelly, and it was like a man looking at his favorite son. All the worry left his face and his smile mellowed and there was a dream in his eyes. "Funny thing, Hamp," Dusty said. "A man works all his life—don't even take time to get married—just to build up a ranch like this. You watch it grow and you feel it killing you and finally you get it to be exactly what you want it to be. Makes you feel almost like a kind of a god, workin' things out with your hands that way." He dug his shoulder blade into the doorjamb. "Then you wake up some morning and you're a sick old man and you know that one of these days you're gonna die—"

"You talk like you been smokin' opium," Hamp Donnelly said.

"I'm talkin' the truth," Dusty said. "I'm an old man, and I've made one little mark on the face of this old earth, and that's Anchor. And if I can't pass Anchor on to somebody that wants it and know for sure they'll keep it, what the hell have I left to the world?" He grinned sheepishly. "Conceit, in a way," he said, "but so is a man puttin' a tombstone on his grave."

"Anchor will stay here," Hamp Donnelly said, "if I have to hold it in place with my hands."

"And you'd by God hold it, too," Dusty said. He grinned that half-shy smile. "You know, it was an old man's idea, I reckon, but I was kinda hopin' you and Ellen would fall in love on sight and be married afore now and then I could lay down and die peaceful and rest like a man ought to. Instead of that, the two of you hit it off like a couple of stray cats."

"Now I know you been chawin' loco weed," Hamp said. "You've got a strappin' big nephew to take over here, haven't you?"

"Paul?" Dusty said. He shrugged his thin shoulders. "Paul wouldn't even come out here to look things over when I asked him to. It was Ellen that come."

"Paul's busy with his work, Dusty," Hamp said. "Ellen told you that."

Dusty Tremaine ran a gnarled hand across his seamed face. "Ellen told me that, all right," he said, "but it so happens it ain't the truth. You forget I was back to Philadelphia last year. I met Paul and I kept a good eye on him, sizin' him up. The only work he ever done was spendin' what little money my brother left him and Ellen."

Ellen Tremaine's voice called from the house. "Uncle Dusty! Dinner is on the table!"

Dusty Tremaine grinned. "Little late in the day for dinner, ain't it, Hamp?"

"They call things different in Philadelphia," Hamp Donnelly said. "They have dinner at night and do without their supper, I reckon."

Dusty Tremaine reached out and gripped Hamp's arm, squeezing it hard. "That's right, Hamp," he said. "They call things different in Philadelphia. That's what worries me." He released his grip and stepped outside, and now it was nearly dark. "Promise me something, will yuh, Hamp?" Dusty said.

"Anything I can, Dusty."

"Keep on eatin' your dinner at noontime and your supper at dark, will yuh?"

"You can count on it, Dusty," Hamp Donnelly said.

Dinner or supper, it was a good meal. Ellen Tremaine could cook. Hamp and Judge Norton had washed up at the bench which stood outside the kitchen door, Hamp acutely conscious of the bruises on his face. The two men came in through the kitchen where Ellen was still busy at the stove. They went into the dining room where Dusty was already seated at the round oak table.

It was a square room with windows on two sides, the pine floors bare and worn, the furniture sturdy and plain. There was an oak sideboard that took up most of one end of the room, and on the other wall was a huge pair of elk antlers which served as a hat and gun rack. Hanging from one prong of the antlers was a gun belt and a holstered and loaded .45, identical to the outfit Hamp Donnelly had taken from his own saddlebags. They were twins, Hamp Donnelly's gun and Dusty

Tremaine's gun there on the elk antlers. Hamp sat down and got to his feet again when Ellen brought a platter of steak from the kitchen.

"Set down before you fall down, Hamp," Dusty Tremaine said. "Pass me the gravy."

"I thought Doc Pettigrew told you to lay off the gravy," Judge Norton said.

"What Doc Pettigrew tells me to do and what I do is two different things," Dusty Tremaine said. "Pass me the gravy."

Judge Norton passed the gravy. "Go ahead and kill yourself, you old fool."

"Some law against it?" Dusty said. He heaped his plate with steak and covered it thickly with the milk gravy. Ellen came in and sat down at the opposite side of the table. She smiled at the Judge and ignored Hamp.

Dusty looked up, and his eyes were tender and lonely and proud. "Ellen," he said, "you're prettier every time I look at you."

Ellen Tremaine took the compliment graciously. "Thank you, Uncle Dusty," she said. "Perhaps it's just the pleasure of being around you that helps my looks."

"Maybe it's the scenery and the good clean air," Hamp Donnelly offered.

"I believe that's so, Mr. Donnelly," Ellen

said. "It is certainly easy to see why Uncle Dusty is so in love with this place."

"There, you see?" Dusty said, squinting his eyes and pointing his knife at the Judge. "Told you she liked the place, didn't I?"

"It's completely heavenly," Ellen said.

Why, you little liar, Hamp Donnelly thought. You hate every inch of it and you know it. He was glad, though, lie or no lie, that Ellen had done everything she could to please her uncle. If you only knew how much Dusty needs you right now, Hamp thought. Dusty Tremaine was a sick man, even if he wouldn't admit it to anyone but himself.

"What happened to Sue?" Judge Norton asked. "I thought she was coming out today."

"Too busy gettin' ready to open the school, I reckon," Hamp Donnelly said.

"I've enjoyed very much knowing your sister, Mr. Donnelly," Ellen Tremaine said.

"Sue's a pretty good girl," Hamp said. He didn't look up from his plate.

"A pretty good girl?" Dusty exploded. "She's just one of the finest girls in the United States, that's all, ain't she, Judge?"

"Sue Donnelly is all of that," Judge Norton said.

Hamp glanced gratefully at the two old men and knew they were both remembering again that day twenty years ago when a horse trader had driven a broken-down wagon into this very ranch yard. A horse trader with a hacking cough and a six-year-old boy and a two-year-old girl. That horse trader had been Hamp Donnelly's father and the two-year-old girl was Hamp's sister Sue. Six months later, still on Anchor Ranch, the horse trader was dead and a bewildered boy of six, twice too old for his age, was wondering what would happen to his baby sister and himself. Judge Norton and Dusty Tremaine, two bachelors, had supplied the answer to that question. They had taken the two homeless kids and raised them as their own. The Judge and Dusty Tremaine were both thinking back. "Sue Donnelly's the finest, that's all," the Judge said again.

"Everyone has been very nice to me here," Ellen Tremaine said. "I especially wanted to have Mr. Rombeck come out and have dinner with us one night before I left."

Hamp Donnelly looked down at his plate, and the Judge hurried with his eating. Dusty Tremaine wiped gravy from his mustache. "You taken quite a shine to that Dallas Rombeck, didn't you, honey?" Dusty asked.

"Why, no, it wasn't that," Ellen said hurriedly. "He knows several people I know back in Philadelphia—he went to school there for a while. . . ." She looked at the three men, searching their faces. "Why? Is there some reason I shouldn't like Dallas Rombeck?"

"I reckon not," Dusty said, resuming his eating. "He's a lawyer, that's all. And no lawyer ain't no damn good."

"Listen, you broken-down polecat," the Judge said. "If it wasn't for me a time or two—"

"Oh, stop it, you two," Ellen said. "Who wants cake?"

The meal finished, Hamp and the Judge went back to the bunkhouse to smoke their pipes. They were silent a long tine, two men who knew each other well enough to share their thoughts without speaking them aloud. In time the Judge knocked his pipe noisily against his heel. "That Dallas Rombeck gets around, doesn't he?" the Judge said.

"Someday," Hamp Donnelly said, "Dal-

27

las Rombeck is going to get around once too often."

"You mean with the Stinson brothers?"

Hamp Donnelly stared into the darkness of the room, and he wasn't thinking so much of Orvie and Tuna Stinson and of how Dallas Rombeck, the lawyer, had defended them in court on several occasions. He was thinking more of his kid sister Sue and of how Sue was falling in love with Dallas Rombeck. . . .

"Dallas Rombeck is just gonna get tangled up in one thing too many someday, that's all," Hamp Donnelly said.

---3

The next two days on Anchor were busy with Ellen Tremaine getting ready for her trip home. Hamp Donnelly saw little of Ellen or Dusty except at mealtime, for they kept themselves closeted in the house with Judge Norton. Hamp used the time to advantage moving a small band of cows down onto the river-bottom grass. He saw that the Stinsons had actually moved their sheep back over into the next canyon, where a small stream fed into the John Day. He was surprised that they had done so without causing any more trouble. He knew the lull was only temporary.

The Stinsons had been in this country as long as Hamp could remember. Until this, their first venture with sheep, they had run a horse ranch at the edge of the Muddy Country. Both the Stinson brothers were mean when they were drunk, which they were often, and they had been in trouble a number of times. They had been arrested twice on suspicion of horse stealing and once for assault with a deadly weapon. Each time the evidence had been insufficient and Dallas Rombeck had defended them successfully.

Hamp let the cows spread out of their own accord along the grassy bottoms and rode back up the slope. On top he reined up, looking out over this land that was the only home he knew, drinking in the beauty of it.

He was worried about Dusty, a worry that was an empty, gnawing pain. Dusty had done everything he had wanted to do in life, and now that he was getting near the end of the road he wanted to close the book with a final chapter that would give his life a meaning and a completeness. Anchor

29

Ranch had been carved out of a wilderness. Something existed where nothing had existed before. It was a monument to one man's determination, and Dusty Tremaine wanted that monument to stand, Hamp knew. With an old man's determination Dusty wanted to die feeling that a hundred years from today Anchor would be known as "the Tremaine place." Hamp could understand how a man might feel that way.

He reined his horse and rode back toward the ranch. He thought of Ellen and wondered about her brother Paul and he thought of how Ellen had changed in these last few days. She had grown more serious as the certain realization grew on her that her uncle expected her and Paul to have Anchor. It was obvious that Ellen Tremaine was ill equipped for the job, and from small bits of conversation he had heard, Hamp was fast suspecting that Paul Tremaine was even more poorly equipped to be a rancher. Dusty must have seen this, but he was stubbornly refusing to admit it. To Dusty, Ellen and Paul were the last of the Tremaines, and that was all that counted.

Hamp looked down on the little ranch headquarters nestled in the cup of the valley and he looked beyond to the towering butte, a landmark on Anchor. "That's where I want you to plant me. Right on top of that butte." Dusty Tremaine had said that a dozen times. "From up there I can keep an eye on Anchor." A welling loneliness flooded Hamp Donnelly. He rode on down toward the ranch, knowing it was time to hitch up the buckboard. Ellen would be leaving within the hour.

At the house Ellen was packing her final bag. Her uncle sat in the chair, watching her, a tired old man who was realizing suddenly that a man's only tie with life was through his children. And Dusty had no children of his own. But he did have Ellen and Paul, his brother's children, and he had Hamp and Sue Donnelly. But Ellen and Paul were his own flesh and blood and that was important to a man. "Doggone, I hate to see you go, Ellen," he said. "It'll be lonesome here without you."

"I hate to leave you too, Uncle Dusty," she said honestly. "But I'll come out again next summer and Paul will come with me."

Dusty Tremaine was quiet a long time. "It would be good for Paul, coming out here, Ellen," he said finally. "A change of scenery. A damn city ain't no place for a young man, Ellen. There's nothin' for him to own, nothin' for him to get his roots into."

She folded a dress carefully and laid it into the bag. "I've thought of that, Uncle Dusty," she said quietly. "It might be the best thing in the world for Paul. I wish he could come out here and be with you for a few months."

"Well, why can't he?" Dusty said eagerly. "Shucks, if he's short of money he don't have to put on with me. I'll send him the fare—"

"It's not that, Uncle," Ellen said. "It's just that Paul should decide things for himself."

"You talk to him about it, anyway," Dusty said. "Hamp could use some help and any man could learn a hell of a lot from Hamp."

She straightened and looked out the window and she could see Hamp Donnelly out by the corral, hitching up the buckboard. "You think a lot of Hamp Donnelly, don't you, Uncle?" Ellen said.

"I couldn't think no more of a man if he was my own flesh and blood," Dusty said. "He's a great man, Ellen. He handles Anchor like it was his own. I never have a worry as long as Hamp's around."

"I'm glad you have him, then," she said.

Dusty looked a little surprised. "Nobody 'has' Hamp, Ellen," he said. "He's part of Anchor, that's all. And Anchor's part of me. We're all one and the same, I reckon. You never could separate us."

She thought of how angry she had been with Hamp Donnelly a time or two and she felt no anger now. She saw Hamp bending to hook the tugs and she could see the breadth of his shoulders, the narrowness of his hips. Behind Hamp she could see the butte that stood between the ranch and the town of Antelope. Yes, she supposed, Hamp Donnelly and Anchor were one and the same, and if she inherited one she would inherit the other. She felt a vague excitement that embarrassed her.

She hated to say good-by. In the month she had been here she had come to love truly this rough, mildly profane, totally direct man who was her and Paul's only living relative. She had found in Dusty a complete sincerity of affection without pretense, an old-world cleavage to family that was refreshing. She came now and kneeled by Dusty's chair and put her arm around his thin shoulders. "Uncle," she said quietly, "don't worry about things."

"Like I told you," Dusty said, "it would be different if you had something to hold you in Philadelphia. But with your daddy and mamma both dead " He placed his hand on her copper hair and pressed her head close to his side. "Sure, you have to give up your friends. But everybody has to give up something in this life to get something better. And you'll make new friends, Ellen. A girl as sweet and pretty as you are will make friends anyplace. And Paul will make friends."

"Paul needs friends, Uncle," Ellen said. "He doesn't make friends easily."

"Your daddy never used to either," Dusty said. "Not when we was kids together. I remember your daddy used to get moody and he'd just set and stare and think. I used to tell him a body could get in trouble thinkin' too hard on a thing."

"Paul's like that," Ellen said.

"Your daddy had brains," Dusty said. "A lot more brains than I had. I had to bend my back and use my hands, but your daddy started out as a timekeeper on the railroad and worked right up into the head office." Dusty was proud, remembering his brother. "That's one thing about the Tremaines, Ellen," he said. "They start something, they stick to it. They don't give up. Paul's a Tremaine, just like you. You and him got the same blood in your veins me and your daddy had and our granddaddy before us. There ain't never been a Tremaine give up on nothin', Ellen."

"I know, Uncle Dusty," Ellen said. "I know that's the way you feel."

"I feel that way because it's the truth."

"Take care of yourself, Uncle, won't you?" Ellen said.

"Me?" Dusty scoffed. "There ain't nothin' wrong with me. I'll admit if I was to try to ride a buckin' bronc or climb the butte yonder like I uster I might get a little palpitations of the heart." They both stood up, and Dusty put his arm around Ellen's shoulder and squeezed her tight. "Doc Pettigrew says if I take it easy I'll live to be a hundred, and Doc's a worse calamity howler than Judge Norton. If Doc says a hundred it means a thousand at least."

"You take it easy, though, and do what he says," Ellen said.

"You sound as bad as Hamp Donnelly," Dusty said disgustedly. "Him sayin' I should say good-by to you here instead of makin' that little ride into Antelope."

"Hamp's exactly right," Ellen said. "Besides, I want to remember you standing there on the front porch waving good-by, and when I come back next year that's where I want to see you for the first time. I wouldn't recognize the house if I didn't see you standing there on the front porch."

"You sure you ain't makin' me stay here just so you and Hamp can be alone to-gether?" Dusty said hopefully.

Ellen laughed and kissed her uncle on the cheek. "How could anyone as romantic as you keep from getting married all these years?" she said.

"I was married to Anchor," Dusty said seriously.

She took his seamed face between her two hands and kissed him on the lips. When she stood back she saw the tears in the old man's eyes and she fought to control her own emotion. "The best good-by is a quick good-by," she said. "Besides, it will only be for a year."

He clung to her hand like a small boy. "Ellen," he said, "if I don't see you and Paul again—"

"Now, Uncle, you stop that talk!" she said, stamping her foot.

"You don't expect your house to burn down, but it don't hurt to plow a firebreak around it," Dusty said. "I'm just sayin' if you don't."

"We went over everything with Judge Norton," Ellen said.

"All right," Dusty said. "You'll have Judge Norton and you'll have Hamp Donnelly to help you along, and you couldn't have two finer."

She heard Hamp Donnelly coming up on the porch. He opened the door without knocking and walked in. "Ready, Miss Ellen?" he said.

"Yes," she said, "I'm ready."

She was wearing a long green traveling dress with a lace collar high around the throat, and now she pulled a perky straw hat down on her copper hair. As she raised her arms to adjust the hat Hamp was conscious of the swell of her breasts and the thin line of her waist. There was a sprig of new freckles across her nose, and where her hair was swept back he could see the white of her scalp contrasted against the faint tan of her cheeks. The tan went well with her green eyes and her copper hair, he thought. . . . She glanced around and saw him watching her. They were both suddenly embarrassed.

Hamp picked up the suitcases, the four

at one time, and went sidling through the door. He loaded the cases into the buckboard and secured a tarp over them to keep out the dust. He rolled a cigarette and stood there waiting, his heel hooked on the hub of the wagon wheel. He saw Dusty and Ellen standing on the front porch. He saw Ellen kiss Dusty, and then she turned and hurried down off the porch and across toward the buckboard, and when Hamp helped her up he saw she was crying. He said nothing but climbed in and started the team, and they took the wagon road that wound up and around the base of the butte and over the crest of the hill where it dropped down to the little town of Antelope.

As he drove away from the ranch Hamp felt an increasing loneliness, almost as if he, too, were leaving Anchor. At the crest of the hill the feeling was compelling in its intensity and he had to admit to himself that he was going to miss Ellen Tremaine. He pulled the team to a stop to let them rest and he turned in the seat. "You can look back at the house from here, Miss Ellen," he said. "If you look close maybe you can see Dusty on the porch."

She took a handkerchief and dabbed at

her eyes. "He's so terribly sweet, Hamp," she said. It was the first time she had ever called him anything but Mr. Donnelly. He found his own first name strangely harmonious to his ears.

"He's the world's greatest man, Miss Ellen," Hamp said. "God busted the mold after He made Dusty."

She felt she had never heard a greater compliment paid any man. "He's really pretty sick, isn't he?" Ellen said.

"Yes, he is," Hamp said honestly. "It wouldn't hurt none if you was to be ready to come at any time."

"He depends a lot on you, Hamp," Ellen said.

"In a way I reckon I depend a lot on him too," Hamp said.

The two of them were there on the seat of the wagon. They turned toward each other and their faces were close, and Hamp saw Ellen's eyes searching his. A dull excitement started inside him and welled upward, and he saw her eyes grow a little frightened. Hamp swallowed hard. "We'd best be going," he said.

"I think we should," Ellen Tremaine said weakly.

Hamp spoke to the team, and they went

over the crest of the hill. From there they could look down on the town of Antelope.

The town was a block of green in the center of a small valley. Overenthusiastic promoters had planted Lombardy poplars twenty years back and now they leaned in the wind, dropping their speckled shade on streets that had never existed. They could see the schoolhouse where Sue, Hamp's sister, taught, and beyond that the roof of Jake Paxton's store, and here and there a few weathered shingles. A man walked down the center of the road between the school and the town, a brown ant on a ribbon of pink.

"I already talked to Perkins at the stage station," Hamp said. "He's got your ticket all ready. You'll take the stage to The Dalles and then catch a boat there down to Portland."

"Philadelphia seems so horribly far away," Ellen said.

"I reckon it is quite a piece," Hamp said.

They drove down the winding road and came to the schoolhouse. "I'd like to see your sister before I leave," Ellen said. She was still frightened at the emotion she had felt there on the hill.

"Sue would like that," Hamp said. 'We'll

stop by the house where she boards and rooms." He nodded his head toward a white frame cottage surrounded by a picket fence. There were hollyhocks in the yard. Ellen saw the sudden frown crease between Hamp's eyes.

There was a red-wheel buggy in front of the cottage gate with a good-looking sorrel mare weight-tied there. "Why, isn't that Dallas Rombeck's buggy?" Ellen asked.

"It's the one he rents," Hamp Donnelly said.

"Isn't that lucky!" Ellen said eagerly. "Perhaps I can say good-by to Mr. Rombeck and Sue at the same time."

"It could be," Hamp Donnelly said. He pulled the team to a stop and got down, ready to help her, but she had gotten down by herself and had already opened the gate and was starting up the walk toward the cottage porch.

A man and a girl came out of the cottage and down off the porch to meet Ellen. The man was young and tall and handsomely dressed, a man with assurance and polish about him. "Ellen!" he said, as if greeting an old friend. "Sue and I were just on the way down to the station to tell you good-by."

41

Sue Donnelly was a small girl with dark hair and blue eyes. There was a beautiful freshness about her. "Hello, Big Brother!" she called across the fence.

"Hi, Pie Face," Hamp yelled back.

"Hamp!" Dallas Rombeck said. "I didn't see you out there."

"I didn't see you either," Hamp Donnelly said.

Dallas Rombeck was between the girls, and now he took Ellen Tremaine's arm and Sue Donnelly's arm and the three of them came down the walk together. It seemed to Hamp that in this instant Ellen Tremaine had changed. She was the Easterner again, and he knew that the next time she spoke to him she would call him "Mr. Donnelly."

"We have plenty of time," Hamp heard Dallas Rombeck say. "Why don't we walk down to the depot? Hamp could bring the wagon and your things along and get everything set for you."

Dallas, Hamp thought, if the lady wasn't catching a stage I'd pile these trunks on your back and make you pack 'em down there one at a time. . . . Hamp climbed into the wagon and was surprised at the way his hands tightened around the lines. "Get up, horses," he said softly. "It ain't none of your fault, the way the world turns."

Hamp was busy at the station, unloading the luggage, talking to Perkins, the agent, making sure all arrangements had been made. From time to time he saw Dallas and Sue and Ellen, but now it seemed as if it were just Dallas Rombeck and Ellen Tremaine. Sue Donnelly was being pushed to one side. She was actually standing apart, away from the other two. Hamp went by her and said, "How's things goin', Pie Face?"

He saw his sister staring at Ellen Tremaine and Dallas Rombeck. Sue seemed to be speaking to herself and not to Hamp. "I'm not sure how things are going," Sue Donnelly said. She sounded bewildered.

"Here she comes!" somebody up the street yelled. The stage swung down the street in a flurry of dust, a half dozen kids running along beside it, trying to keep up. Every dog in town started barking, and men came out of the Elkhorn Saloon and gathered around the station.

While the horses were being changed Hamp Donnelly helped Ellen into the stage. For a moment he stood there, his head thrust in through the window in the door. "Have a good trip, Miss Ellen," he said. Then, awkwardly, "I'll miss you."

"Thank you, Mr. Donnelly," she said. "I'll miss you too.

We should have started talking this way a month ago, he thought savagely. He searched her face, looking for that certain softness he had seen in her eyes there at the top of the hill. For a second it was there and then it was gone and she leaned past Hamp and waved to Dallas Rombeck. "I'll call on the Tiltons as soon as I get home, Mr. Rombeck," she called to Dallas.

"Wonderful, Ellen," Dallas Rombeck said. He had taken off his beaver hat, and the sun was on his face and it glinted against his black, curly hair. Sue was standing by his side. "Give the Tiltons my best regards, won't you?" Dallas said, cupping his hand by the side of his mouth.

"I certainly will," Ellen Tremaine called back. "And I'll write you and let you know how I find them all."

"And be sure and write your uncle Dusty," Hamp said gruffly.

Ellen looked at him, startled. "Why, of course I will," she said.

"I want to tell you something, Miss Ellen," Hamp Donnelly said seriously.

"This is big country, and once in a while you find a man as big as the country itself. Your uncle Dusty is like that. A really big man is sometimes pretty soft inside."

"Really, Mr. Donnelly, I have—"

He interrupted her. "I know it's different here," he said. "I know Antelope ain't Philadelphia, but folks feel the same inside. This country is maybe a little hard to get used to, but once you do get used to it there's nothing in the world can ever take you away from here again."

The driver came stomping out of the stage office, slapping his gloves against his knees. "Get your punkin head out of the window, Donnelly," the driver yelled, "or I'll yank it off for you."

"Reckon you can handle that fresh team all right?" Hamp bantered back.

"I can pop a fly off your tail with a bull whip too," the driver said, climbing up. "Hiyah! Hiyah!"

The stage lurched and the dust swirled. Hamp Donnelly stood there, waving, and he could see Ellen Tremaine leaning out the window, waving back. After the stage was gone he could still see her face. Hamp turned, and Dallas Rombeck and Sue Donnelly were walking up the street, arm

45

in arm. Hamp felt that sinking twinge of loneliness. That girl got under a man's hide. He shrugged. Might as well have a drink and get it out of his system. Hamp started across the street toward the Elkhorn Saloon and he saw the two riders swing in from around a building and dismount directly in front of him. He hesitated just a second. It was Orvie and Tuna Stinson.

4

The presence of Orvie and Tuna Stinson didn't change Hamp Donnelly's decision to have a drink. He was not a man who would pick a fight for no reason, but experience had taught him that in this country there was no sense trying to avoid one if it was coming.

He went into the saloon, blinking a moment in the semidarkness after the glare of the street, and he saw Ned Crockett, the town marshal, standing at the bar talking to Clete, the bartender. The marshal was a young man, lean and weathered, tough, his eyes much older than his years. Ned Crockett and Hamp Donnelly had been friends all their lives. "Hello, Law

Dog," Hamp said. "Caught any criminals lately?"

"How could I?" Ned Crockett said, grinning. "You ain't been in town."

Hamp glanced around the room. He saw the Stinson brothers at a table in a far corner. They were sitting with Boyd Novis, the sheepman, which confirmed Hamp's previous suspicion that Boyd Novis was backing the Stinson brothers' venture into the sheep business. Hamp turned his back on the trio and motioned for a bottle. If the Stinsons wanted any trouble here they'd have to start it themselves.

"How's Sue?" Ned Crockett said. He was trying to make his voice sound impersonal.

"Why don't you ask her, Ned?" Hamp said.

"She seems pretty busy lately," Ned Crockett said.

"A man could always break up that kind of business, couldn't he?" Hamp said.

Ned doffed his glass. "If Sue ever needs me, I'm here," he said. "She knows that."

"I know it too, Ned," Hamp said.

"Hey! Donnelly!" Tuna Stinson's voice jarred through the room, loud and coarse. Tuna was a big man and he looked enough like his brother Orvie to be his twin. He had

47

the same muddy eyes and, like Orvie, he wore his hair long. "Have a drink, Donnelly?" Tuna Stinson said.

"I'm having one," Hamp said. He raised his eyes and looked in the back-bar mirror. Tuna had pushed his chair away from the table and was leaning back, his thumbs hooked in his gun belt. Hamp could see Boyd Novis sitting there nervously, an extremely small man with a stubble of blue-black beard on his jowls. A few years back Boyd Novis had been one of the first sheepherders in the country and now, according to rumor, he was close to a millionaire. Money had given him an arrogance and an insolence that were out of keeping with his size.

"I wanta talk to yuh, Donnelly," Tuna Stinson said.

"Go ahead and talk," Hamp said. "I'm listening."

"Brother Orvie tells me you think you own both sides of the John Day," Tuna said.

"Brother Orvie is mixed up as usual," Hamp said.

"Watch it, Hamp," Ned Crockett said. "No trouble now."

Clete, the bartender, started mopping the bar vigorously. Hamp saw with satisfac-

48

tion that one of Orvie Stinson's eyes was black and nearly closed. The big man's upper lip was split and swollen. Orvie stood up. He was unsteady on his feet, and Hamp knew the man had been nursing his hatred with whiskey. "You callin' me a liar, Donnelly?" Orvie Stinson blurted.

"Not right now, Orvie," Hamp said. "But I've had occasion to."

"Damn you, Hamp," Ned Crockett said quietly, "I told you to watch it."

Orvie stood there swaying on his feet, his eyes mean. "I got a notion to pistol-whip hell out of you, Donnelly," Orvie said. "I got a notion to teach you some manners."

"You get those notions when you got your big brother to back you up, don't you, Orvie?" Hamp said.

Ned Crockett moved away from the bar, and Boyd Novis got up from his place at the table. Boyd Novis's voice was thin, his black eyes bright. "I was trying to talk business with these two gentlemen, Donnelly," Boyd Novis said. "Why don't you go someplace else for your drink?"

"Why don't you, sheepherder?" Hamp said.

He saw the color form two red patches on Boyd Novis's high cheekbones. Orvie

49

Stinson reached down and took a shot glass from the table. He downed the drink quickly, his eyes never leaving Hamp Donnelly's face. Hamp had faced a man who was itching for a gun fight before; he knew he was facing one now. "Where'd you leave your gun, Donnelly?" Orvie said. There was perspiration on Orvie's upper lip.

"Shut up and set down, Orvie," Tuna Stinson said unexpectedly. He got up and took his brother by the shoulder and forced him into a chair. "Mr. Novis's time is valuable."

Orvie Stinson sat flatly in his chair and continued to stare at Hamp Donnelly. "Next time don't leave your gun in the wagon, Donnelly," Orvie said.

Hamp felt Ned Crockett's hand on his arm. "Have your drink, Hamp," Ned Crockett said.

Hamp and the marshal turned their backs on the trio at the table. "Damn you, Hamp," Ned Crockett said. "Someday I'm gonna have to lock up either you or the Stinsons to stop a killing."

"Could be," Hamp said.

"What's the trouble now, Hamp?"

"The Stinsons are running sheep on their place. The way I see it, those sheep must belong to Boyd Novis, and to me that means Novis is reaching out for more graze. You and me have both watched him take over two thirds of this country, Ned."

"He hasn't tried to take over Anchor, has he?" Ned Crockett said logically.

"Not yet," Hamp said. "But he will if he has the chance."

"All right," Ned Crockett said. "When he tries it, cut loose your dog. Until that time, behave yourself. I'd put you in the hoosegow as quick as I would anybody else."

"I expect you would, Ned," Hamp said. He clapped his friend on the back. "I got to be gettin' back to the ranch. Be seein' you."

Hamp went out into the sun and swung down the board sidewalk toward Jake Paxton's general store. Once he glanced toward the stage road where it wound up toward Shaniko and he thought of Ellen getting farther and farther away from him. He turned in at the store and helped himself to a handful of crackers out of the barrel and leaned against the counter, tossing half crackers at his mouth. "Get that wire for me, Jake?" he asked the storekeeper.

Jake Paxton hitched his black sleeve guards and peered through his steel-rimmed glasses. "Yeah, I got it," he said. The storekeeper had a way of fidgeting, digging his elbows into the counter. He looked at Hamp's bruised face and spit into the coffee can he always kept near his feet. "Orvie Stinson was in here an hour or so ago," Jake said.

"It's not surprising," Hamp said, "this being the only store in Antelope."

"Orvie looked like he slid down a cliff on his face," Jake said.

"The hell you say?" Hamp said. "Better set me out about six sacks of rolled barley. I'll drive around in back and pick 'em up."

"Six sacks barley," Jake said, writing it on a pad. He moistened the pencil with the tip of his tongue. "That Miss Ellen went back to Philadelphia, did she?"

"She headed off in that direction, sure as hell," Hamp said. "Give me three boxes of .45 center fires."

Jake Paxton's eyes were beady bright as he reached down to get the cartridges. "Snakes bad out along the river this year, are they?" he said.

"I don't know," said Hamp. "Should they be?"

"Orvie Stinson bought a couple of boxes of shells for that new .30-.30 of his."

Hamp felt the tightness across his shoulders. "The gun won't shoot without shells," Hamp said. "Give me a two-bit sack of that squaw candy you got in the jar there. Dusty likes it."

"How is Dusty?" Jake asked.

"Pretty good," Hamp said. "Get that barley out on the platform, will yuh?"

"Sure, Hamp," Jake Paxton said. "Sure I will." He scurried down the counter like a little brown squirrel, then stopped and half turned. "I ain't a man to cause trouble, Hamp," he said. "I didn't mean nothing, telling you Orvie Stinson bought those .30-.30 shells."

"That's all right, Jake," Hamp said. He walked out of the store and crossed the street to where he had left the team and wagon. As he tooled the team around in the street he saw Orvie and Tuna Stinson and Boyd Novis come out of the saloon and walk up toward the two-story hotel. They didn't enter the front door but went up the covered stairway that ran up the outside and led to the second floor. A man's got to be mighty thick with Boyd Novis before he gets invited up to the great man's room, Hamp thought to himself.

He drove the team around to the back of

Jake Paxton's store and loaded the two rolls of wire and the six sacks of barley. Jake handed up a box, and it held the cartridges and the rock candy. "I didn't mean to pry into your affairs, Hamp," he said.

"Jake, that's a damn lie," Hamp said, grinning. "You know you did." He slapped the lines and they left dust streaks on the backs of the matched bays. Turning the team, Hamp drove down the main street past Dallas Rombeck's law office and took the road that led to Anchor.

The wagon road lifted into the barren hills, winding and dipping and always climbing. The red dust clung to the rims of the wheels and fell loose and left a pale pink cloud behind the wagon. Hamp drove slowly, his eyes squinted against the bright light that reflected from the blue sky and burned back from the brown grass. Streamers of dust trailed from the stunted sage and drifted into the scatter of juniper. The land was alive with a brittle dryness, spiced with tarweed and cured grass.

This was home. This was the beginning of Anchor. This was one man's dream, and it had to remain the way that man had planned it. Hamp crossed the ridge by the butte and looked down at the cluster of buildings that was Anchor. "I'll take care of things for you, Dusty," Hamp said silently. "I promise you I'll do that much."

Hamp was glad to see that Judge Norton was at the ranch when he drove into the yard. He pulled the wagon up at the granary and unloaded the barley and rolled off the wire. Then he unhitched the team and with the tugs hooked up he led them over to the horse trough and let them drink.

The Judge and Dusty came out of the house, Dusty walking with that peculiar, rolling gait. The two men were nearly the same age, but the Judge was straight and wiry, Dusty was old and bent. The weather and the land take a lot out of a man, Hamp thought to himself. When a man builds a ranch he leaves a lot of himself in it.

"Did she get away all right, Hamp?" Dusty called.

"Everything eggs in the coffee," Hamp said. He took the team to the barn and un-harnessed, and Dusty and the Judge followed him. The two old men stood there, leaning on the manger, watching Hamp.

"Tell me," Dusty said finally. "Just what do you think of her?"

"She's a real Tremaine, Dusty," Hamp

said. "Did you see how quick she took to everything? She handles a horse like she's been riding all her life. She can read your earmarks two miles off."

Dusty Tremaine laughed like a pleased kid. "There you are, Judge, you see? You damned old calamity howler."

"Dusty, she's a woman," the Judge said. "You can't expect a woman to just pitch in and take over full charge."

"Why in the damn hell do you always talk like Paul don't even exist?" Dusty exploded. "It's my nephew I'm leavin' this ranch to. How many times I have to tell you that?"

"All right, all right, calm down," Judge Norton said. "Don't bust a blood vessel."

Dusty's grin was as quick as his temper. "But that Ellen's a fine girl, ain't she, Hamp?"

"She sure is, Dusty," Hamp said.

"Pretty, too," Dusty insisted.

"Damn pretty," Hamp admitted, and suddenly his memory of her eyes and of her lips was too vivid for comfort and he was remembering her leaning out the stage window, waving to him.

"If I was a young buck your age—"Dusty began.

"Look, padre," Hamp said, clapping his

boss affectionately on the shoulder. "I got a lot of cows to chouse and in another month at most we got to get a haying crew in and get our hay up for winter."

"And you've got a band of sheep right across the river from you, too, don't forget that," Judge Norton reminded in his sepulchral voice.

Hamp Donnelly shook his head. "They moved 'em back, Judge."

"How long you expect 'em to keep back?" the Judge asked.

"I wouldn't know, Judge," Hamp said. "But I'll keep an eye on it." He looked at Dusty and grinned. "You better get back to the house and take a cat nap like Doc told you."

"What the hell am I?" Dusty said. "A two-year-old?"

"You act like one sometimes," the Judge said.

The Judge and Hamp stood and watched Dusty limp toward the house, muttering to himself. It made Hamp sick to see Dusty old like this. The Judge was standing there staring after his friend, and when he spoke it sounded as if he were talking to himself. "You can't talk to the old coot," the Judge said. "You can't do a thing with him."

"Don't try, Judge," Hamp said. "If he wants Ellen and Paul Tremaine to run Anchor, then that's the way it will be."

"Do you think Ellen and Paul can do it?" the Judge asked, his lawyer logic toning his voice.

"They'll have to do it, Judge," Hamp said quietly.

"And what happens when Orvie and Tuna Stinson start crowding sheep in on them?" the Judge said.

"Well, then I reckon I'll just have to be there to crowd them sheep right back," Hamp said. He took the boxes of .45 shells he had bought from Jake Paxton and went to the bunkhouse.

-----------------------------------5

The buildings of Anchor, surrounded by the inevitable windbreak poplars, lay on a bench overlooking the river valley. Besides the house there was a small bunkhouse, a large barn, and a horse corral. There was a mowing machine and a hay rake between the corral and the bunkhouse. The ground around the house was hard-packed and bare, and at times the winds swept in across the vast plain from the Columbia River to the north, sheeting the country with ice.

It was not a vast holding, but over the years Dusty Tremaine had been able to pick up a parcel here and another there until now the land which comprised Anchor was owned land rather than leased, as so many larger operations were.

At first this had been cattle country, but gradually the sheep had moved in, starting with Boyd Novis's first band. One by one the cow outfits sold out or converted to sheep, and one by one Boyd Novis managed to buy them up until Anchor was the last of the independent cattle outfits, a small island of land surrounded by sheep. Anchor still ran cattle, a good grade of Durham, descendants of cattle brought to Oregon by the first settlers. To the north was the Columbia port town of The Dalles, and down the river at its junction with the Willamette was the fast-growing city of Portland. There was a market for beef, and Anchor was a good living for anyone.

It was home to Hamp Donnelly, the only home he had ever known, and he felt the strong tug of it as he rode across the rough acres, handling the ranch as if it were his own.

It was two weeks now since Ellen Tremaine had left for the East. Hamp Donnelly missed her, and he was surprised that he did. He hadn't had much time to think of women in his life.

The sun was just up and it was blood red on top of the butte that looked down on Anchor. Hamp rode down the slope and into the long valley rich with meadow hay. In another few weeks he would scout up a haying crew. Until Dusty's sickness Dusty and Hamp had been able to handle the entire operation of the ranch except at haying time, when they hired three or four men. During the severe winters the cattle drifted down into the canyons, and the cured meadow hay, hauled out to them, carried them through until the first spring grass was green. It was an old pattern and a never-ending one, and to Hamp there was comfort and permanence about it.

Hamp hadn't seen the Stinsons again since that meeting in the Elkhorn Saloon in Antelope. He had seen their sheep every time he rode up on the hill, but the Stinsons were keeping their sheep well back from the river, and there was worry even in that fact. It was like a cloud of impending trouble, a storm cloud that lingered, holding a promise of destruction, a power that was always there.

Hamp rode through the valley and into a canyon where he picked up a couple of horses that had strayed. Hazing them along in front of him, riding slowly, he headed back to the ranch. As he topped the hill and looked down at the ranch house he saw the buggy pulled up in the yard.

He thought at first it was Dallas Rombeck's rig, but it surprised him that it should be there so early. Sue was coming out tonight to cook supper for him and Dusty and the Judge, and Dallas was driving her out. Hamp didn't approve of Sue's friendship with Dallas, but he knew Sue better than to try to forbid her seeing the man. Sue had a mind of her own and she could be as stubborn as a bull calf. He hoped sincerely that this romance between Sue and Dallas would wear itself out. He had always expected Sue to marry Ned Crockett. He still hoped it would work out that way, but it would have to be Sue who made the decision. Hamp was an independent man. He respected other people's independence.

When he reached the corral he saw that it was neither Rombeck's rented buggy nor Doc Pettigrew's, the two rigs that would be most likely to be here. He turned the stray horses into the corral and started toward the house, an annoyed frown on his face. It wasn't good for Dusty to have too much company.

Halfway to the house Hamp heard Dusty's voice charged with anger. "Get out of my house, you filthy sheepherder. You're stinkin' up the place!" The door flew open and Boyd Novis backed out onto the porch.

The little sheepman was shaking his fist under Dusty's nose. "I came out here friendly, on a strictly business proposition, Dusty Tremaine, and I expect to be treated with respect—"

"I'll treat you with respect, you land-grabbin' sheepherder!" Dusty yelled. "If you was one inch bigger than fryin' size I'd bust yuh in the nose! Now get out of here before I take down my gun and pistol-whip yuh!"

Boyd Novis turned, nearly colliding with Hamp. His face was blood red, his black eyes alive with anger. He climbed into his rig and jerked savagely on the lines, spinning the buggy out of the yard. Dusty Tremaine stood there in the doorway, his face white, his hands trembling. Suddenly his shoulders sagged and he gripped at the doorjamb for support. Hamp stepped forward swiftly, put his arm around his boss, and half carried him back into the house.

"What are you doing, getting yourself riled up like that?" Hamp said. He felt a swift, consuming anger toward Boyd Novis.

"That damn miserable sheepherder," Dusty said. He was gasping for breath. "He come here tryin' to buy Anchor from me, wavin' his damn sheep-smellin' checkbook under my nose—"

"What's the sense getting so excited about it?" asked Hamp.

"The guts of the man," Dusty said, "thinking I'd let sheep run over my grave."

"All right," Hamp said, "calm down. You told him it wasn't for sale and that's that."

But that wasn't the end of it, and Hamp knew it. Boyd Novis had never failed yet to get any piece of land he went after, and now he was after Anchor. Hamp thought of Ellen and Paul and wondered what would happen if Boyd Novis came to them and made a substantial offer to buy Anchor when Ellen and Paul were in control. "Where's that medicine Doc told you to take?" Hamp said.

"I threw the damn stuff out," Dusty said. "It tasted like hell."

Hamp Donnelly shook his head. He left Dusty there on the couch and went to the kitchen to get a glass of water. As he came back through the dining room he glanced at the elk horns and saw Dusty's gun hanging there in its holster. It was always loaded, always ready. The gun was a lot like Dusty, Hamp thought. He came back in and handed the glass of water to his boss.

"You stretch out there and take it easy," he said. "Sue will be along pretty soon."

"That's good," Dusty said, heaving a deep sigh. "The only thing wrong with me is I been eatin' too much of your cookin'."

They heard a horse outside, the sound of a man dismounting. Hamp glanced out the window. "Here's the Judge," he said. "I'll let him sit here with a club and keep an eye on you."

"Damn calamity howler," Dusty said. "He had me dead and buried six months ago."

Hamp laughed. Judge Norton came in without knocking. He took a quick look at Dusty and said, "What's the old fool been up to now?"

"He tried to whip Boyd Novis," Hamp said, "but Boyd was too big for him. Hell, Boyd comes clean to Dusty's shoulder."

"Stinkin' sheepherder," Dusty said.

"What was Boyd Novis doing here?" the Judge asked.

"Tryin' to buy Anchor, what do you think?" Dusty said.

The Judge glanced at Hamp, catching the implication, and Hamp saw the worry in the older man's eyes. "What's he want to do?" the Judge said. "Own the whole state of Oregon?"

"Looks like it," Hamp said. "It's time he finds parts of it ain't for sale." He pushed his hat back. He wanted to get out where he could keep an eye on things, knowing Boyd Novis would move swiftly. "I'm gonna ride up there on the hill and take a look at that little bunch of cows I been doctorin' for screwworm," he said. "Tell Sue to go ahead and fix supper. I'll be back before dark." He went back to the corral where his horse was tied. He tightened the cinch, patted the horse on the flank, and swung into the saddle in a long, liquid motion. It was ten in the morning, and the sun was beginning to reach its warmth.

Up at the crest of the hill there was a small flag of dust where Boyd Novis's buggy had disappeared over the hill on the way back to Antelope. Hamp chuckled, thinking of the way Dusty had told Novis off, but it was a chuckle with no mirth in it. If Boyd Novis had decided he wanted Anchor, he wouldn't give up with just one cash offer.

Hamp liked these leisurely afternoons alone. Sometimes as he rode he felt as if there were no one else in the world but himself and no other place in the world but this place. He rode through small bands of cattle, glancing at them with a practiced eye, and once he stopped to let his horse rest. For a long while he sat in the shade of a boulder, smoking a cigarette, squinting out across the blue and tan distance. Far below him the John Day River was a silver streak through a valley of green.

To his left he could see two loops of the wagon road to Antelope, and to his right was the more direct five-mile-shorter horseback trail that ran from Antelope, through Anchor, and over to the river. A puff of dust on this trail caught his attention.

Hamp stood up and watched the trail and he saw a man on horseback riding at a full run. The distance was too great for him to determine the identity of the man, but he decided it was one of the Stinson boys. Only a Stinson would be fool enough to mistreat a horse that way. It jerked his thoughts back to Boyd Novis and the Stinson sheep, which, Hamp knew, had been placed there deliberately to harass a sick old man. Hamp put out the cigarette and mounted and rode on, keeping in the shadow of the rim-rock.

The sun was dropping rapidly into the fir-covered slopes of the Cascades, and the snow fields of Mount Hood and Mount Jefferson were alive with light. Hamp watched the road and saw no sign of Sue and Dallas Rombeck, and he wondered why. It was about time to go back to the house.

He had crossed beyond the short-cut trail from town now and he turned back toward it, intending to take that trail back to the ranch to save time. He had just reached the trail when he saw Sue and Dallas Rombeck coming from town. He hailed them. "I figured you'd drive out," Hamp said.

"I felt like riding for a change," Sue said, waving to him. Her hat was back on her shoulders, secured by a chin strap. Her dark hair was loose around her face. She was wearing a divided skirt, knee-length boots, and a man's shirt. Dallas was dressed in town clothes as usual. He rode amazingly well.

"I'll ride on in with you then," Hamp said. He nodded to Dallas.

They rode along together, saying little. "Dusty had a bad spell," Hamp said finally, directly to Sue. "Boyd Novis was out and made an offer to buy Anchor."

"I can imagine how Dusty took that," Sue said. "Honestly, sometimes I feel someone ought to run Boyd Novis out of the country."

"That's the penalty of being successful," Dallas Rombeck said. "Not many people like a really successful man."

"Depends on what you call success," Hamp Donnelly said. "Boyd Novis is still a sheepherder to me."

Dallas Rombeck laughed. "You'll have to admit the man has certainly made money."

"It hasn't changed him none," Hamp said.

They came to the fork where the main trail went on to the river and a dimmer, less used trail branched off to the left and led down to Anchor headquarters. As they topped the rise they could look straight down into the river valley at the exact spot where Hamp and Orvie Stinson had had their fight. A hard knot formed in the pit of Hamp Donnelly's stomach and his hands gripped the pommel of his saddle.

Sue Donnelly saw her brother's face. A faint bleating of sheep lifted up to them along with the staccato barking of dogs. A band of sheep was moving down toward the river, moving swiftly, and as they watched two men on horseback galloped into the band and forced the first of the sheep into the shallow stream.

"Go on to the house," Hamp Donnelly said tightly.

The color had drained from Sue's face. "You can't go down there alone, Hamp."

"Go on to the house, Sue," Hamp said. "You go along with her, Rombeck. And don't let Dusty know anything is wrong."

———————————————6

The first wash of blazing anger in Hamp Donnelly changed to a cold determination. A showdown with the Stinsons had been coming from the moment they started running sheep. He knew that and he had expected it, and in a way he was glad it was here. He didn't stop to consider the fact that there were two men down there with those sheep and he was alone any more than he would have stopped to consider that the temperature was twenty below zero and cattle were piled against a drift fence. There was a job to be done.

He rode down the broken slope and the river was there below him, wide and shallow at this point. On the slopes running down to either side of the river were rain-washed gullies and scattered boulders. The bleating of the sheep was clear now, as was the constant yammering of the dogs. Hamp rode as fast as the terrain would allow, straight down toward the river. He was nearly to the stream before he became aware of the fact that there was only one man on horseback there. He reined up sharply and glanced around, trying to determine what had happened to the other man.

He could see Tuna Stinson out in the middle of the river. Tuna was apparently trying his best to turn the sheep back onto his own land. Hamp reached the flat and spurred his horse to a gallop, and now Tuna turned and came up from the river. He was waiting on the Anchor side of the stream, his horse dripping water, when Hamp slid to a stop.

Tuna was unarmed and he had both his

hands folded on the saddle horn. "All right, Tuna," Hamp Donnelly said. "I told Orvie what would happen if those sheep crossed over."

"Hold on now, Donnelly," Tuna Stinson said. "They ain't crossed yet and I'm doin' my best to turn 'em back. Me and Orvie had to be away for a couple of days and the sheep drifted, that's all."

"That's a lie, Tuna," Hamp Donnelly said. "I saw you and Orvie pushing them."

Tuna Stinson's eyes were wide with innocence. "Me and Orvie? Hell, man, Orvie ain't even in the country. He went up to The Dalles for a couple of days."

"Who was with you then?" Hamp demanded.

Tuna Stinson spit between his horse's ears and looked Hamp straight in the eye. "Not a soul, Donnelly," he said. "Just me and the dogs."

"Stinson," Hamp Donnelly said, "you've been planning this trouble for a month and you know it."

"I can't figger what's eatin' on you, Donnelly," Tuna Stinson said. "The sheep drifted down here and I'm doin' my best to drive 'em back. You can see that with your own two eyes. Me personal, I don't want no

71

trouble and I never have wanted no trouble. Just because there's bad blood between you and Orvie—"

The main part of the band was still on Stinson grass across the river. The dogs were working out in the shallow water, nipping at the few sheep still in the river, trying to turn them. To a casual observer Tuna Stinson was doing exactly what he said he was doing—trying to avoid trouble with his neighbor. Hamp's eyes swept the rocks across the river, searching for some sign of Orvie. He knew he had seen two riders.

"Look, Donnelly," Tuna Stinson said. "I mortgaged myself to the hilt to buy these sheep. You must have figgered that out for yourself. I can't afford to have no trouble with 'em. I'm sorry this happened, if that's what you want me to say. Give me a hand and we'll put 'em back on my own creek and keep 'em there."

Tuna Stinson was too agreeable, too contrite. This was part of a plan and Hamp Donnelly knew it. At the moment Tuna Stinson wasn't showing all his cards, and the certain knowledge that that was so made Hamp want to jerk the big man out of the saddle and shake the truth out of him. But it was like a poker game. If Hamp wanted to see Tuna's cards he would have to string along. "All right, Stinson," he said. "Let's turn 'em back. If you've got a trick up your sleeve just remember I've got a gun here and it's loaded."

"Hell, Donnelly," Stinson whined, "I ain't got no trick."

The two men worked side by side on horseback there in the river, turning back the sheep. Hamp was alert to every move Tuna Stinson made, but apparently the big man had no intention of starting anything. If Tuna had a hide-out gun Hamp couldn't spot it. Tuna worked hard. He seemed grateful for Hamp's help.

But Hamp had ridden here certain that this was the showdown. His muscles and nerves, everything, had been ripe for it. The reaction he had received from Tuna Stinson left him completely at a loss. It was an old gun fighter's trick, he knew, this knocking a man off guard with the unexpected. But Tuna was not armed, so that meant Orvie would get into this.

The last of the sheep were out of the river when Tuna Stinson jerked his horse so hard it reared. Hamp saw it and his hand dropped swiftly to his gun, and then Tuna was fighting his horse, looking back across the river. "What is this, Donnelly?" Tuna said thickly. "I told you I didn't want no trouble!"

Hamp followed the big man's nervous gaze and saw the three riders coming down the Anchor slope toward the river. They were Judge Norton and Dallas Rombeck, and the third man was Dusty Tremaine. Hamp cursed furiously under his breath. The last thing in the world he wanted was for Dusty to know anything about this until it was all over. Dusty had been strictly forbidden to ride a horse, and beyond that, he couldn't possibly stand the excitement of trouble. "You stay here, Tuna," Hamp said. "I'll ride across and tell 'em it's all right."

Tuna Stinson was nervous as a cat. "How about these sheep?" he said. "I can't move 'em back alone."

"I'll give you a hand later," Hamp said.

Hamp splashed across the river just as Dusty, Dallas, and the Judge reined up on the other bank. "Dusty!" Hamp exploded. "What the hell's eating on you?"

"I told him there wasn't any need for him to come down here," Dallas Rombeck said.

"You half-witted shyster," Hamp raved. "I told you I didn't want Dusty to know any-thing about this, didn't I?,'

Dusty Tremaine leaned across his saddle horn, his face thin and hard. He had strapped on his .45 and it hung heavy against his thigh. "Who owns this ranch, Hamp Donnelly?" Dusty said, and Hamp heard the old whip of authority he hadn't heard for years. "If there's trouble on Anchor," Dusty said, "it's my trouble. Nobody has to handle it for me."

"There's no trouble, Dusty," Hamp said. "The sheep drifted. Tuna's trying to move 'em back and I offered to help him."

"Since when does an Anchor hand herd sheep?" Dusty Tremaine said. "I'll handle Tuna Stinson!" He drew the .45, pulled it to half cock, and rolled the cylinder to a full chamber. "I don't need no help." He spurred his horse and rode into the river.

Hamp wheeled his own mount and blocked Dusty's way. "Put that gun away, Dusty," he said tightly, "or I'll take it away from you."

The old man's eyes were blue and bright and the seams were deeper in his face. "You ain't man enough, Hamp Donnelly," he said. "Get out of my way."

Hamp could see the tension in Dusty Tremaine's face, the slow, pulsing heartbeat in the hollow of his throat. A feeling

75

of near terror racked Hamp as he remembered what the excitement with Boyd Novis had done to Dusty. Here was a thing Hamp Donnelly couldn't fight; sickness was trouble in the dark, a thing that couldn't be seen. "Dusty, please," he said.

Dusty had the .45 in his hand. He waved the barrel. "Get out of my way, Hamp."

Hamp had to decide quickly between what he could see here and that hidden enemy, Dusty's sickness, and his decision was that it would be less strain on Dusty to let him ride across and talk to Tuna than it would be to stop him and hold him here. "All right, Dusty," Hamp said. "If I go with you."

The two men rode across the river side by side, and as they came up the shelving bank Tuna Stinson was sitting his saddle, his hands shoulder-high. "I'm unarmed," he said. "Donnelly knows that."

"I got a notion to gut-shoot yuh anyhow," Dusty said.

"Damn it to hell," Tuna said, "I was only tryin' to do what was right."

"You never did right by no one in your life, Tuna Stinson," Dusty Tremaine said, "and you know it. You drove them sheep down here and you drove 'em deliberate and you done it because Boyd Novis told you to do it."

"Boyd Novis?" Tuna said. "What's he got to do with it?"

"I ain't playin' no question-and-answer games with you, Tuna," Dusty said. "I run Novis off my place this morning, so he give you orders to give me sheep trouble. I wasn't born yesterday."

"I ain't got nothin' to do with Boyd Novis," Tuna protested.

"Me and Hamp will give you a hand movin' those sheep back this time," Dusty said. "But the next time them sheep get near Anchor graze I'll club every damn one of 'em if I have to do it singlehanded, and you can tell Boyd Novis so."

Dusty dropped his gun into its holster, and Hamp saw the quick change in Tuna Stinson's eyes. There was a look of cunning and satisfaction there now, and Hamp felt a deep disgust along with his apprehension. A man had to be pretty low to crawl and squirm the way Tuna was doing. Pretty low or pretty foxy . . . "Go on back across the river and wait, Dusty," Hamp said. "I'll see Tuna moves the sheep."

"I'm still boss of Anchor," Dusty said. "I'll give the orders."

The tone of Dusty's voice gave Hamp a thrill. It was hard to believe that this man was sick. He had been confined for a long time and now he was out in the open on a horse with a gun belt around his waist, and it was like the old days. This moment was all the years Dusty had spent building up Anchor, a moment of pride and confidence when a man was king of his own destiny. Since the beginning of his sickness Dusty had said a hundred times that this was the sort of medicine he needed, this was the tonic. At this moment it was easy for Hamp to believe that this might be so. "All right, boss," Hamp said, "but keep back. This jigger's got an ace up his sleeve, and I aim to make him show it."

The bleating and bewildered sheep piled on each other and milled and split off into small bands and turned back on themselves. The dogs worked magnificently. In time Tuna pulled up his horse and dismounted. "A man can do better with 'em on foot," he said.

"It's bad enough for me to be this close to sheep," Dusty said, "but damned if you'll get me on foot." Hamp Donnelly felt the same way. He kept working his horse around, keeping himself between the slope

78

and Dusty. Orvie was up there someplace, Hamp was sure.

The ground lifted sharply here, and a hundred yards above them up the slope was a cluster of boulders higher than a man on horseback. Hamp kept watching those rocks. Tuna was on foot, yelling at the sheep, working wide, away out to one side, leaving Dusty and Hamp together, directly below the cluster of boulders.

A few of the sheep had wandered up toward the rock pile, and when they were near there they stopped stiff-legged, broke, and ran back down the slope. At that second Hamp's suspicion was confirmed and he knew what had happened to Orvie Stinson.

Hamp drew his gun and glanced at Tuna. He saw Tuna run far to one side, then stop and wave his arms. "Dusty!" Hamp yelled, forcing his horse against Dusty's mount. "Get out of here!" He lashed out with his reins, splashing Dusty's horse across the eyes. The animal reared and plunged. The crack of a rifle filled the narrow valley of the John Day.

The lead burned fiercely close to Hamp's face. He wheeled his horse, and from the corner of his eye he saw Dusty's horse plunging and bucking. He could see Dusty's death-white face. Hamp threw up his gun and fired three wild shots toward the rocks. Token shots without a chance of hitting anything, but maybe they would drive Orvie to cover. The rifle smashed again, but the plunging horse made a poor target and the bullet went wide.

Over the echo of the gunshots Hamp heard the wild shout from across the river, and he knew that Judge Norton and Dallas Rombeck were splashing across. Hamp turned his gun toward Tuna, fighting to keep from pulling the trigger. Tuna was still standing away off to himself, his hands high above his head. "I'm unarmed," he kept yelling. "I ain't got nothin' to do with this!"

Hamp heard Judge Norton's voice. "Dusty! For God's sake, help Dusty!"

Hamp wheeled that way. A riderless horse was splashing across the river. Dusty Tremaine was stretched out on the ground, still as death, a cocked .45 clutched in his bony hand.

7

There was a wild confusion of sound, sheep bleating, men shouting, dogs barking. Hamp started up the slope toward the rock pile, and at that moment if he could have put his hands on Orvie Stinson he knew he would have killed the man with his bare hands. The stark violence of his feelings startled him.

He looked back, and the Judge and Dallas were still a good hundred yards from Dusty. Dusty was crawling along on his stomach, trying to get to his hands and knees, failing. He was a perfect target if Orvie decided to fire again. Hamp threw himself from the saddle and ran back down the slope. He dropped to his knees and lifted Dusty's head in his arms. "Easy, Dusty," he said. "You're all right now. Take it easy."

"It was a trap," Dusty gasped. "We should have shot Tuna when we seen him."

"Easy, Dusty," Hamp said. He felt the slight weight of the old man in his arms and he stood up, lifting Dusty, carrying him as he would have carried a child. There was a bitter, hard lump in Hamp Donnelly's throat, and his eyes stung like fire. He stood there holding Dusty Tremaine in his arms and he looked at Tuna Stinson, a big, hulking man with tawny eyes and shoulder-length hair.

Tuna's face was white. "I didn't have nothin' to do with it, Donnelly," Tuna said.

Hamp Donnelly's lips were pulled tight against his teeth. "I'll kill you for this, Tuna," he said. "I'll get Orvie first and then I'll come for you." He turned his back on Tuna Stinson and walked stiffly toward the river, carrying Dusty Tremaine in his arms.

Dallas Rombeck had gone back and caught Dusty's horse, and now the young lawyer was leading the animal across the river. Hamp looked at the horse and saw the empty saddle, the slapping stirrups, and it was like a symbol to him. Dusty Tremaine's empty saddle. "We got to get him back to the ranch," Hamp said. "I'll take care of things here later."

It was an endless ride, that ride back to the ranch. A ride with moments of hope and moments of complete helpless despair as Dusty Tremaine rallied for a moment and then collapsed and had to be held in his saddle. In those swift moments of change Dusty Tremaine was king of Anchor, as indestructible as the butte which stood behind the house. And again he was an old man, eroded and worn by time and weather, just as some of the land itself was eroded and worn.

Hamp Donnelly didn't speak a word. He rode close to Dusty, his right arm supporting the old man in the saddle. Hamp would allow neither Dallas Rombeck nor the Judge to touch Dusty until they were back at the house. When Dallas came forward to help, Hamp pushed him aside and waited for the Judge. Dallas had not been a close friend to Dusty. He had no right to help now. Together Hamp and the Judge carried Dusty into the house.

The big bare living room with its oak and leather chairs and stone fireplace was starkly familiar to all the men. They carried Dusty to his own bedroom, and as Hamp removed the rancher's boots he kept thinking of the old saying: "He died with his boots on." The saying had never meant anything before. Just a comic saying. He tried to force the phrase out of his mind, but it was still there. If Dusty had to go, perhaps this was the way he wanted it. With his boots on. He had gone down fighting

83

for the one thing that meant most to him in life. Anchor.

Sue Donnelly moved in and out of the room, asking no questions, quietly efficient. Hamp didn't see her. The driving, consuming hatred for Boyd Novis and the Stinsons and what they had done was a bright physical pain inside Hamp Donnelly's chest. He reached down and unbuckled Dusty Tremaine's gun belt. "You won't need this for an hour or so, boss," Hamp said.

Dusty Tremaine was smiling. His face was dead white and his breathing was rapid and shallow. Hamp felt hot tears welling behind his eyelids. He took the gun belt and hurried out of the room, and he stood in the dining room a long time, looking out the window, across the land that was Anchor. He buckled the gun belt and hung it carefully on the elk horns where it had hung so long. The gun was still loaded. It was ready for use, the way Dusty had always kept it.

He heard Dusty's voice, weak, unnatural. "Judge?"

"Yes, Dusty?" Judge Norton said.

"Get those papers again, Judge," Dusty said. "We got to change 'em."

"There's no need of that now, Dusty," the

Judge said. "You rest. Sue is fixing you something in the kitchen."

"Damn you. Judge Norton," Dusty said, "you'd argue with a man when he's dyin'. Get those papers!"

"Now who's a calamity howler?" Judge Norton said. His voice sounded broken. "You're too damn mean to die."

"Get those papers," Dusty said. "What the hell am I payin' you for?"

"Paying me?" the Judge said. "You haven't paid me a fee in twenty years."

"Because yuh ain't been worth it," Dusty said. "But I'll pay yuh for this one. This one has to be right."

The pain in Hamp Donnelly's chest was shaped like an anvil. It was impossible for him to take a deep breath. The point of the anvil would puncture the breath and then the breath would explode and choke him and would come back through his nostrils in short gusts of ammonia, stinging and burning and making his eyes water. He hurried out of the dining room, out through the kitchen and the back door, past the bench where the bucket and basin stood, past the spot that was always damp where he and Dusty threw their wash water. He stumbled blindly toward the bunkhouse and nearly collided with Sue. He had completely forgotten that she was here.

She gripped both his arms and held them. "Hamp," she said softly, "get hold of yourself."

For a moment he couldn't answer her, and then all the emotion that was in him broke and he put his arm around his sister and held her fiercely close to him and his fingers entwined in her hair.

She felt the complete grief of her brother and it frightened her. She had always leaned on him, thought of him as a man who could never waver or change his pace regardless of what happened. Now she realized that a man's emotion could be directly in ratio to his strength. It was terrifying to see him break, and at the same time she knew she was being drawn more closely to him than she had ever been before.

And Hamp, after that first blind second, became self-conscious of the fact that he had turned to someone for help. But for that moment he had needed Sue and he had known, too, that there were times when a man needed a woman.

"It was Orvie and Tuna," Hamp said finally. "If anything happens to Dusty—"

"Don't think about it now, Hamp," Sue said. "Please, not now." She moved away from him. "I'll do what I can."

"He wants to be alone with the Judge right now," Hamp said.

"Then I'll wait until they're finished," Sue said.

Hamp saw her hurrying toward the house, a small girl, beautifully formed, a girl completely mature. Hamp was fearfully proud of her. He watched her and saw Dallas Rombeck come around the house. Dallas walked over to Sue and put his arm around her, and Sue hid her face against Dallas Rombeck's chest. A complete emptiness and loneliness settled on Hamp Donnelly and wouldn't go away. A woman could need a man, too, he saw. A man who was not her brother.

Hamp went out to the bunkhouse. He sat down on the bunk. He took off his hat and he sat there, his face buried in his hands. It was an hour before any organized thought crossed his mind. During that hour there were patches of memories floating like small wisps of morning fog across a meadow. Wisps driven away finally and completely by the bright sun of decision.

He stood up then, a tall, lean man, wind-burned and saddle-hard. A man with blond hair and keen blue eyes and a certain undeniable harshness to his features. He knotted and unknotted his big hands and then, looking out the east window, he could see the slope running down to the river valley, and now the emotion had run its course and he could think with a crystal clearness.

There was never any doubt in his mind that it was Orvie Stinson who had fired those rifleshots. The Stinsons were not men who made major decisions on their own. The crimes they had committed were petty crimes. Boyd Novis had ordered them to move those sheep, and Orvie, knowing Hamp Donnelly would be there to try to stop it, had probably decided on his own to set the ambush. The shots had been intended for him, Hamp knew. The fact that Dusty had been along had only confused the issue and probably helped to save Hamp's life. If Orvie and Tuna had planned this as an ambush for Hamp, they had certainly not expected Dusty to get out of his sickbed and be there.

It angered Hamp to think of how he had ridden so completely into the trap, but as he thought back he saw there actually would have been no other way. A poker game, he thought savagely. You have to pay to see a man's cards. But this time there was going to be a final pay-off after the game.

Bit by bit he reconstructed everything that had happened this afternoon. Outside the sun dropped behind the towering butte and the familiar shadow came and lay softly across Anchor Ranch. Hamp remembered the countless times he and Dusty Tremaine had climbed that butte. He remembered the table-flat top and he remembered Dusty setting his horse, his hat in his hand, the wind in his hair. Dusty looking down at the ranch he had built with his own hands. Dusty saying, "When I kick the bucket, Hamp, be sure I get planted up here where I can keep an eye on things."

A man could say a thing like that and it was a joke. It meant little, talking of death when everyone is well and death is a distant acquaintance who has called once or twice and then gone away. A man could joke about death. But when death was close, there in the house, it was no longer a joke. It became the biggest event in a man's life. Even bigger than his birth, because before a man was born he was nothing, but when a man died he had been, and he could be remembered. He could leave a part of himself behind. A man like Dusty could leave Anchor as his monument.

It was dark now and the evening had passed into night. Hamp had eaten no supper. No one had. He sat there on the bunk, completely tired with a fatigue he had never known, the fatigue of emotion. He heard the slow crunch of boots on gravel and knew Judge Norton was coming to the bunkhouse. The sound of the footsteps told him all he needed to know.

The door opened and Judge Norton came in. He looked thin and tired and a little bewildered, an old man with white hair and a drooping white mustache. Odd, but he looked like Dusty Tremaine. . . . "Dusty's gone," Hamp Donnelly said. It was not a question.

Judge Norton nodded his head slowly.

"It was Orvie Stinson killed him," Hamp Donnelly said. His voice was flat, metallic, and it jarred through the narrow room.

"You take it easy, Hamp," Judge Norton said.

"It was Orvie Stinson," Hamp said again. His voice was soft now and he was saying it to himself. He knew as certainly as he was sitting here what he had to do.

The Judge was talking, telling Hamp everything Dusty had said. Perhaps the Judge had been talking a long time. Hamp didn't know. The Judge was telling Hamp every word of his final conversation with Dusty and it was important, but Hamp was only half hearing. All that legal talk. It meant nothing. Hamp knew what Dusty wanted. He didn't have to hear this legal talk. "I would have called you, Hamp," the Judge said. "Dusty wanted to see you, but it was too late."

"It's all right," Hamp said. "I'll be seeing Dusty again. Often. I'll see him up there on the butte. Every time I look that way." He stood up and made a cigarette. The flare of the match fanned against the lower half of his jaw. It made his face appear harsh and cruel.

"The first thing is to get word to Ellen and Paul," the Judge said. "You want to take care of that, Hamp?"

Hamp Donnelly shook his head. "That's your work, Judge," Hamp said. "I got my own to do."

The Judge laid his hand on Hamp Donnelly's arm. "Think it over, Hamp. You can't let nothing happen to you now. Ellen and Paul Tremaine will need every bit of help they can get. Dusty wanted you to stay on here and get things started. He made that plenty clear. And if Ellen and Paul tried to sell Anchor you'd have to be here then, I told you that—"

"You better get on to town and get Perkins out of bed and send that telegram," Hamp Donnelly said. "As it is, it will be a month or more before Ellen and Paul can get here." He thought a minute. "Any legal reason I can't go ahead with work on the ranch get the haying started?"

The Judge looked closely at Hamp. "Haven't you been listening? I explained that to you. You're in full charge here."

"Then go on and send your telegram," Hamp Donnelly said.

Hamp pulled his hat tightly down on his head. He took a sheepskin-lined coat from a peg on the wall and shrugged into it. The night was cold. He moved closer to the light and took a new box of .45 cartridges from the small drawer of the pine table. He loaded the gun carefully, five chambers, and then one by one he filled the loop of the cartridge belt with brass cartridges.

"Think it over, Hamp," the Judge said.

"I've thought it over," Hamp said. "I've thought it over careful. I want Dusty to sleep good up there on the butte." For just a second his voice broke. "Judge, you take care of the funeral. Will you do that for me?"

"Of course I will, Hamp," the Judge said.

"And tell Sue not to worry."

"I'll do that," the Judge said.

The Judge was an old man. He had seen a lot of trouble in his time. He knew when it was useless to argue further with a man. The Judge watched the door close softly, and out there in the darkness he could hear Hamp catching up a fresh horse, saddling. He heard Hamp's heavy weight swing into the saddle.

Judge Norton sat there alone. He wanted just a little time before he went back in the house. Once inside the house, he would have to console Sue and he would have to try to explain to her why Hamp had gone. But perhaps that part of it wouldn't be too difficult. Sue was a product of this country and in a way she was part of Anchor, just as Hamp was part of Anchor. She had been as close to Dusty as Hamp had been. No, Sue would understand why Hamp had to ride tonight. A disturbing thought tormented Judge Norton. Suppose it was Ellen Tremaine in that house tonight? Suppose he had to explain to Ellen Tremaine why Hamp Donnelly had to kill a man?

Judge Norton wished he could cry. That was one nice thing about being young. A young man could cry. He got up and cupped his thin hand around the lamp chimney, and the blue veins on his hands were bluer. He blew out the light, and as he stepped out into the darkness he heard Hamp Donnelly riding up the trail that led over toward the river and from there to the Stinson place in the canyon beyond. Judge Norton looked at the same stars that Dusty Tremaine had looked at for so long, and he smelled the breath of the land, the same land Dusty Tremaine had worked and loved.

The Judge started walking toward the house.

─────────────────────────────────8

By the feel of the air it was near five o'clock in the morning. Hamp Donnelly rode, a darker mass of gray in the grayness that covered the land. He crossed the river, and it was silent and black, the smell of it thick in his nostrils. He was taking his time now, a man who knew exactly what he would do and how he would do it. There was no need to hurry. Orvie and Tuna Stinson would not leave the country. That would make their guilt too obvious.

From up on the ridge a man could see the world, but here in the canyon, with the confines of the hills around him, Anchor became a pin-point focus of land, and Hamp Donnelly's thoughts were focused as sharply as were the limits of his vision.

He felt no effect at all from his lack of sleep. Rather it was as if the morning had awakened him not merely to a new day but to a new life. He felt the new responsibility he would have to face, a maturing feeling that sharpened his decision.

He stopped at the river and let the horse drink, and he stayed there a long time, a broad-shouldered man hunched in his saddle, his hands folded on the pommel, the collar of his sheepskin coat turned up to meet the brim of his hat. The current of the stream broke around the horse's forefeet with a small burbling sound. Far in the distance a lone coyote clamored at the dawn and a sheep dog answered with a warning challenge.

This was the time of morning that was

neither tomorrow nor yesterday, and it was hard to separate the present and the future from the past. Hamp glanced up at the barren hills above him, sharp and blue now in the coming light, and Dusty Tremaine was everywhere, the spirit of the man remaining in this place even though the body was gone.

Twenty years slipped back, and Hamp Donnelly was remembering that first day when he had come to Anchor. They had driven down the road from Antelope that day, Hamp Donnelly, his father, and Sue, a child in arms. Hamp hadn't thought of his father for a long time, but now suddenly the picture of that man was crystal-clear. A thin-faced man with a hacking cough and eyes that never settled on anything. A man who grinned too easily and scratched his shoulder and ducked his head when he talked.

There was no clear-cut beginning to Hamp Donnelly's life as he remembered. His father had bought horses and sold them, and the family moved constantly from place to place. At first that had seemed of little importance, but as Hamp Donnelly grew older he realized that the movements of his father and mother were not always of their own choice. A tricky horse deal here, a bill left unpaid there. They would move along.

Hamp knew that his mother had been very young and very pretty. He remembered that she had a quick, sharp way of talking, a way of nagging at a man. He knew now for sure that when men had gathered around the broken-down wagon his own mother had been more of an attraction in this womanless land than had the horses his father had to sell.

They camped in some abandoned shack as often as not, and sometimes they pitched a tent and many times, deep in the night when Sue, the baby, was sleeping soundly, Hamp Donnelly, six years old, had lain awake listening to the harsh voices of his mother and father. He had never felt any great affection for either of them; he had never known security. Without knowing it, these two people had shaped Hamp Donnelly's life. He had decided early that he wanted to possess every quality they lacked.

It had been no great surprise to him that final morning when his father had said bluntly, "Your maw lit out with another man. I reckon we can get along just as well without her."

Hamp Donnelly had known from that moment that it would be his job to look out for Sue. He still felt that strong, protective interest. And from then on they wandered all over the state of Oregon. French Prairie, where the farmers had first settled and the houses were strong and the land good. The central backbone of the state with the tall snow-capped mountains and the scent of pines. The coastal plain with the dairy herds and the foreign-sounding people, the constant rain and an old man's growing cough. He remembered the startling width of the Columbia River, and to this day the river seemed like an ocean to him. Then the long trip across the mountains, the miles of wheat, the tremendous cattle ranches, the first band of sheep. And Hamp's certain knowledge that this land was to be his home.

They traveled with horses always, and Hamp Donnelly developed a way with horses. And one day, with a broken-down wagon, a perfectly contented two-year-old girl, and three horses that were not worth selling, the Donnellys had come to Anchor. Hamp Donnelly remembered the first time he had seen Dusty Tremaine.

Twenty-odd years ago. Twenty years

made a lot of difference in a man. Dusty's hair had been dark then, his eyes keen and penetrating. Dusty had looked at Hamp Donnelly's father and Hamp had felt shame, for he had known immediately that here was a man the horse trader couldn't fool. Dusty listened quietly while Hamp Donnelly's father told his story, bidding for sympathy, claiming he was sacrificing the horses to feed the kids. And when Hamp's father was finished Dusty Tremaine had smiled, and it still seemed to Hamp it was the warmest smile he had ever seen.

"I can't use the horses, good as you say they are," Dusty had said. "But a man gets lonesome out here, and I sure would admire to set and talk with yuh a spell and hear about where you been. You'd favor me if you and the kids would stay and eat with me."

That was the beginning. The Donnellys had come to Anchor. They never left it. Within six months Hamp Donnelly's father was dead. Hamp knew at the time he should feel deep grief. He didn't. He went to Dusty Tremaine like a man would go, for he felt he was a man. "Me and my sister will move along," Hamp had said, and he tried to spit across his lips in exactly the way Dusty

Tremaine would have done it. "When I get some money I'll send it along. We don't want to cause you no bother."

He remembered Dusty Tremaine's eyes, no sympathy in them, no pity. A man's eyes looking at another man. "You mean you'd walk out on me right when I need yuh?" Dusty had said. "It's near hayin' time and I counted strong on you drivin' one of the wagons."

"I reckon I could stay a spell then," Hamp Donnelly had said. He remembered how he had felt strong and good because Dusty needed him, and he had hitched his belt with the flat of his hands, a habit he had acquired from Dusty Tremaine. Hamp had walked away from the house, a grown man at the age of six.

Twenty years ago . . . The scarlet of dawn was staining the ridges now, but the blue shadows of the hills still lay in the river. Funny how time could pass and a man would think nothing of it until one day he awoke suddenly to the realization that something had ended and something new was beginning. Hamp Donnelly rode slowly up the hill, and it was as if he had gone back through the years and was back at the point where Dusty had said, "I need you." Dusty

Tremaine still needed him, Hamp knew. Now it was Ellen and Paul, but that was the same. It was still Dusty.

Hamp dismounted there by the rocks and in the half-light he examined the ground and saw the marks where a horse had stood. There were two empty .30-.30 cartridge cases there in the dust, shiny, new, smelling of powder. He picked them up and dropped them absently into his shirt pocket. Orvie Stinson had a .30-.30 rifle. So did a lot of other men, but that didn't matter. Hamp mounted and took the trail down the canyon toward the Stinson place. The sun was not up, but its promise was strong here on the east slope.

The Stinson place lay in a small valley. Hamp Donnelly reined up and looked down on it, a place as unkempt as its owners. There was no smoke coming from the wired-up stovepipe. Hamp loosened his gun belt and then took off his coat, folded it carefully, and tied it behind his saddle. He rode down the slope openly to the small meadow, and he followed the rail fence of the horse corral. The scent of tarweed and dry grass was in the morning.

He rode near what appeared to be a tool shed dismounting there, keeping the shed between himself and the house. There was still no movement from the house. Hamp measured the distance from the tool shed to the cabin with his eye, then ran across the open space and flattened himself against the windowless side of the cabin. He stood there a moment, breathing heavily. There was perspiration on his face, and he wiped it away with his sleeve.

Hamp turned and pounded with his fist on the wall of the cabin. He called Orvie's name, and the echo came back twisted and hollow. There was no sound from inside the cabin. Once again Hamp called and got no answer, and then, gun in hand, he walked around to the front of the house. He kicked open the front door. The cabin was empty:

Hamp backed away from the shack, turning to avoid a broken saddle astride a sawhorse. From the looks of it, the saddle had been there all winter. He went to the barn and saw there were no saddles on the pegs there, and he knew for sure then that Tuna and Orvie were gone.

He holstered his gun and went to the horse corral, where he examined each horse carefully. He found the one that had been ridden recently, and it could be the horse he had seen running along the trail yesterday afternoon. The horse had been ridden desperately hard. Its coat was still swirled and marred by excessive sweating, and its flanks were cut deep with spur marks. The caked blood was still there.

Hamp went back to the house and beyond to the well. He had to prime the pump. He drank two dippers of water and then he pumped a third and dashed it on his face, wiping his face dry with his sleeve. He mounted then and turned his horse back. After a day like yesterday the Stinson boys would feel the need of whiskey, Hamp figured. The closest place to get whiskey was in Antelope. Hamp Donnelly rode his horse that way.

It was hot that day in Antelope. Hamp Donnelly rode past the schoolhouse. He thought of Sue and how she had made a place for herself teaching here. He caught himself comparing Sue Donnelly with Ellen Tremaine, and it was a difficult comparison, for the two girls had nothing in common. He rode past the school and into the town, and now he rode slowly, keeping his horse in check, his senses alert to every sound and every movement.

The town was old and weathered before

its time, a collection of false-front buildings and tired cottages badly in need of paint. Behind the town the low brown hills ran up to the stunted sage and juniper of the Bake Oven Plateau. The town was awake, but it was quiet. Hamp rode past Jake Paxton's store, and his eyes searched the hitch rail in front of the Elkhorn Saloon. There were no horses tied there.

At the far end of the block was the low, squat building where Ned Crockett, the marshal, had his office. He owed it to Ned to tell him, Hamp figured. He wouldn't let Ned stand in his way, but Ned had a right to know about it. Hamp rode past the saloon and dismounted in front of the marshal's office. He rattled the door and saw that the place was empty.

Two men Hamp knew came out of Jake Paxton's store. They glanced down the street and saw Hamp and they ducked back inside the store. In a matter of minutes the entire feel of the town had changed, and Hamp Donnelly knew that everyone knew why he was here. That was all right, he thought to himself. It meant that Orvie Stinson was here ahead of him.

Hamp missed no detail of that town as he walked down the sidewalk, keeping close to the buildings. He had seen this place five hundred times or more, but now he was seeing it for the first time. That space between Jake Paxton's store and the harness shop . . . Exactly six steps wide. The flat roof of the bakery across the street, the false front projecting above it. A man with a rifle could hide there. Hamp passed Paxton's store, walking slowly, and he knew men were inside, staring out at him. He turned at the end of the street.

He crossed the street openly and started down the other side. He stopped directly across from the Elkhorn Saloon. The door of the saloon was open and Clete, the bartender, was standing just inside. "Is Orvie Stinson in there?" Hamp Donnelly called.

"He ain't in here, Hamp," Clete called back. "I'll swear he ain't."

"All right, Clete," Hamp said.

Hamp moved on down the sidewalk, the muscles in his face pulled hard and tense. Across the street was the two-story Antelope Hotel where Boyd Novis had a room. Hamp appraised the building carefully, seeing the covered stairway that led up the outside of the building to the second story. His eyes traveled along the row of windows until he found Boyd Novis's window. No, he thought, Boyd Novis is too smart for that. Boyd Novis wouldn't let Tuna and Orvie come there.

He turned and had taken three steps when he heard Clete's voice, high and thin with terror. "Look out, Hamp!"

A rifle smashed, and the lead splintered into the wall of the building near Hamp's head. Hamp turned and dropped to one knee, his gun flashing from its holster. He saw the glint of metal there in the open end of the outside stairway at the side of the hotel. He fired once and threw himself behind the fire-water barrel that stood on the sidewalk. The rifle answered and the lead punctured the barrel. Water spurted out into the thirsty dust.

Someplace near a woman screamed. Dogs started barking, and a horse tied in front of Jake Paxton's store broke its reins and went running down the street directly between Hamp and the hotel.

There was a thud of boots inside the covered stairway. Hamp Donnelly ran across the street, running brokenly, his gun in his hand. He reached the bottom of the stairway, and there in the semi-darkness he could see Orvie Stinson at the top of the stairs. Orvie was beating on the door, yelling, "Novis! Let me in!"

Boyd Novis's thin voice came from beyond the door. "Stay out of here! I don't want any part of this!"

"Down here, Orvie," Hamp Donnelly said quietly.

Orvie Stinson turned. He had lost his hat, and his long hair was hanging around his face. The big man threw the rifle to his hip and fired. The bullet cut a furrow down the steps. Hamp Donnelly fired back.

Orvie Stinson fell heavily. He hit against the side of the covered stairway and then he tumbled down the steps. He rolled halfway down before his hands clutched out in front of him and broke his momentum. His body lay sprawled there on the stairs. The rifle slid on down the steps, bouncing with dead thuds, and it clattered out onto the sidewalk Hamp Donnelly holstered his gun. Someplace the woman was still screaming. She was screaming, "Why doesn't someone stop it?"

A half dozen men came out of Jake Paxton's store. They stood there on the sidewalk, staring at Hamp Donnelly. At the far end of the street two riders came into the town. One was Ned Crockett, the marshal.

He had Tuna Stinson with him. Hamp Donnelly stood there and waited. He saw that Tuna Stinson was wearing handcuffs.

Ned Crockett dismounted slowly. He walked toward Hamp Donnelly, a man who had been his friend for a long time. "Give me your gun, Hamp," Ned Crockett said.

Hamp drew the gun and offered it, butt first. "I looked for you, Ned," Hamp said. "I wanted to tell you about it."

"The Judge told me when he came in to send the telegram," Ned Crockett said. "You should have waited, Hamp. You can't take the law in your own hands this way."

The marshal went into the covered stairway. In a few seconds he was back. He kicked Orvie Stinson's rifle to one side. "You're under arrest, Hamp," Ned Crockett said.

"All right," Hamp said. "If that's the way it has to be."

"That's the way it has to be," Ned said.

Hamp turned and saw Tuna Stinson sitting there on his horse, his wrists handcuffed together. He saw Tuna glance at the marshal and then at Hamp and then at Brother Orvie's rifle lying there on the sidewalk. A bellow of animal rage broke across Tuna Stinson's lips. He twisted himself sideways and lunged out of the saddle, landing on his feet. He came at Hamp running, his arms up. Tuna's arms crashed down, and the steel handcuffs bit into Hamp's shoulder, knocking him sideways. Hamp came rushing back in, and Ned Crockett was there between the two men. The marshal's gun barrel cracked against the side of Hamp Donnelly's head. Hamp staggered back, and the marshal's cocked gun was digging deep into Tuna Stinson's middle. "That's enough, Hamp," Ned Crockett said.

"Take those irons off him," Hamp said. He was breathing deeply and there was a trickle of blood on the side of his face. "It's got to come sometime, Ned. Take the irons off."

"I said it was enough," Ned Crockett said softly. "You're under arrest, the two of you."

"I'll get you for this, Donnelly," Tuna Stinson said. "If it's the last thing I do, I'll kill you for it!"

"I'll be waiting for you, Tuna," Hamp said. "I'll be watching my back and waiting."

Tuna Stinson glanced into the open stairway and saw Orvie's body sprawled there.

The sound Tuna made in his throat was both a sob and a cry of helpless rage.

——————————————————————————9

The jail was small. It was stuffy and hot and smelled of disinfectant. Ned Crockett came in from the outer office carrying a tray of food covered over with a dish towel. Hamp Donnelly got up from the bunk. He stretched his arms and came over to the barred door, grinning at the marshal. "I'm sick of looking at you, Ned," he said.

Ned Crockett clicked his tongue against his teeth. "After only two weeks?" the marshal said. "I've had some customers in here as high as three months. They learn to love me."

"How about my next-door neighbor?" Hamp said, nodding his head toward Tuna Stinson's cell. "Has he learned to love you yet?"

"You're cute, Donnelly," Tuna Stinson said through the bars. "You're just as cute as hell. When I get out of here—"

"When you get out of here, Tuna," Ned Crockett said, "you're gonna take a nice, long trip. I'll get you a floater out of this town if it's the last thing I ever do."

"The trial ain't until this afternoon, Crockett," Tuna Stinson said. "I'll let the Judge decide if there's a charge against me. Shove that slop in here."

"I wish it was slop, Tuna," Ned Crockett said. "It happens this jail feeds good."

"Maybe Tuna would like some sheep meat," Hamp said.

"Shut up, Hamp," Ned Crockett said. "Nobody asked you."

Hamp could hear Tuna eating noisily in the next cell. He uncovered his own plate. There was steak, hot biscuits, fried potatoes, and a cup of coffee. Hamp sat down on the edge of the bunk and rested the plate on his knees. "Won't you join me for lunch, Marshal?" he said.

Ned Crockett took keys from his pocket and unlocked Hamp's cell door. "Come out in my office and eat it," Ned said. "You've got company."

"Hey!" Tuna Stinson yelled. "How about me?"

"You've got company too," Ned Crockett said. "I'll send him in."

Hamp stood up, and he felt his appetite leaving. "Judge Norton?" he asked.

"If it was," Ned said, "I'd send him in here. It's Sue."

Hamp felt a sudden bone weariness. "Look, Ned," he said, "why don't you tell her we'll talk about it later?"

Ned Crockett looked steadily at his friend. "Stinson's lawyer wants to talk to him," Ned said. "They've got a right to privacy. Come on out in my office."

Hamp shrugged and followed the marshal through the outer door. He left his plate in his cell. He was no longer hungry.

Sue Donnelly was sitting at the marshal's desk. She was wearing a sunbonnet tied under her chin. She looked very young. Dallas Rombeck was standing behind her chair. "All right, Rombeck," Ned Crockett said. "You can go talk to your boy."

"Hamp," Dallas Rombeck said, "I hope you understand how these things are. There's nothing personal about it—"

"Go talk to your boy, Rombeck," Ned Crockett said The marshal looked at Sue Donnelly, and the strong affection he felt for her was there in his eyes. He motioned Hamp toward a chair. "You've got ten minutes, you two, if you want it," he said. "Behave yourselves or I'll come in here and knock your heads together." He went out-

112

side and sat down in a chair on the sidewalk directly in front of the office door.

Hamp Donnelly tried to grin at his sister. "Everything going all right out at the place?" Hamp said.

"I suppose it is," Sue said. She still didn't look at her brother. "Judge Norton hired some men to start on the hay. I cleaned the house."

"Has the Judge heard for sure when Ellen and Paul will be here?" Hamp asked.

"At least a couple of weeks yet, I suppose," Sue said. She was twisting a small white handkerchief in her hands. The handkerchief tore. Quick tears came into Sue Donnelly's eyes. She turned then and faced her brother for the first time. There was defiance in every line of her pretty face. "Well, go ahead and say it," she said.

"Not much to say, Sue."

"Can't you understand that Dallas is a lawyer?" Sue said. "It's his business to defend people who are in trouble."

"I didn't say it wasn't, Sue."

"You might as well make up your mind to it, Hamp," Sue said. "I love Dallas and he loves me. We're going to be married."

Hamp Donnelly leaned across the desk and put his hand on his sister's arm.

"Honey," he said softly, "all in the world I ever wanted for you was the best. Sometimes, maybe, people think with their emotions instead of with their heads."

"How would you know?" she flared. "You've never been in love."

He wondered. He thought of Dusty Tremaine and of Anchor and he looked at Sue, this girl who was both a daughter and a sister to him. He managed to smile.

She was crying openly now, and he got up and put his arm around her and held her close. Over her shoulder he could see the crowd of people who had come to the town to attend the court hearing. "I'm worried, Hamp," Sue said, sobbing against his chest. "Suppose they charge you with murder?"

"They won't," Hamp said. "You run along and I'll buy you a good supper tonight at the hotel."

"I'm having supper with Dallas," Sue said. "If they turn you loose we can all three eat together."

"We'll see," Hamp said.

Dallas Rombeck came from the cell block. He stood there a second, his hat in his hand, his dark wavy hair precisely in place, the black string tie knotted with a

114

studied unevenness. "I'm sorry you feel this way, Hamp," Dallas said.

"I don't feel any different than I ever did, Rombeck," Hamp said. "See you in court." He turned and went back inside. He let himself into his own cell and closed the door.

"Get everything all settled, Tuna?" Hamp called through the bars.

Tuna Stinson was sitting on the edge of his bunk. He kept clenching and un-clenching his big hands. He turned his shaggy head slowly and stared straight at Hamp Donnelly. Hamp could see the burning hatred in those tawny eyes. "When it's settled between you and me, Donnelly," Tuna Stinson said, "it won't be in no courtroom."

"I reckon that's right, Tuna," Hamp said.

Judge Norton's fingers drummed nervously on the long oak table. He glanced down toward where Tuna Stinson sat, sullen and belligerent, and he saw Dallas Rombeck leaning back in a Douglas chair, young, smiling, and confident. It had been a long time since Judge Norton had taken a case in court. He felt a little rusty, a little nervous. He leaned forward and tapped Hamp on the shoulder. "Remember now," the Judge said. "The thing that has to be decided today is whether or not you can be charged with murder. If you are arraigned for murder—"

"Now, Judge," Hamp said easily, "it's your job to remember all that."

"Damn it, man," the Judge said, mopping his forehead. "You could be in trouble, you know. A murder charge is a lot more serious than an accessory-to-the-crime charge, and that's the most we can hope to get against Tuna—"

"What kind of a haying crew did you get, Judge?" Hamp said. "Look like a pretty good outfit?"

"Hamp, to hell with the haying crew," the Judge said.

Hamp leaned back in his chair and looked out at the courtroom. "I'd like to have the hay all put up when Ellen and Paul get here," he said. "Hear any more from them?"

The law, Hamp Donnelly decided during the next three hours, was not a business to his liking. Witness after witness said the same thing over and over. Hamp kept watching Sue sitting there with her head down, pulling at that torn handkerchief, and he kept hearing Dallas Rombeck. He knew that Dallas was only doing his job—that this was all supposed to be completely impersonal. There's one part of being a lawyer I could never quite make work, Hamp thought to himself.

The witness was Jake Paxton, the store-keeper. Dallas Rombeck had his hands on his hips, under his coattails. He kept walking back and forth. "And you say, Mr. Paxton, that on the day of this alleged killing Orvie Stinson came to your store and bought a box of .30-.30 rifle cartridges?"

Jake Paxton looked like a small field mouse sitting in the witness chair. "I don't want to cause nobody no trouble," Jake said. "I got a business—"

"Just answer yes or no, please," the presiding judge from The Dalles said, rapping his gavel.

"He bought 'em," Jake Paxton said.

"How many boxes of .30-.30 shells do you sell in a month, Mr. Paxton?" Dallas Rombeck asked.

"A case or better, I guess," Jake Paxton said weakly.

"Would you say a .30-.30 carbine is a

common gun, Mr. Paxton?" Dallas pressed. He was smiling now.

"I'd say it was," Jake Paxton said. He glanced at Hamp and then glanced away.

"Then a box of .30-.30 shells wouldn't be too unusual a purchase for a man to make, would it, Mr. Paxton?"

"No, it wouldn't be," Jake Paxton said.

A big blue fly droned around Hamp Donnelly's head. He slapped at it two or three times. Judge Norton frowned and shook his head. A moment later Hamp brought his hand down with a resounding slap, and everyone in the courtroom jumped. "Got him," Hamp said, pleased. He brushed the dead fly from the table.

It was Dr. Pettigrew on the stand.

"As a doctor of medicine," Dallas Rombeck said, "you treated the late J. P. Tremaine?"

"I took care of Dusty, if that's what you mean," Doc Pettigrew said.

"He had a serious heart condition, did he not?" Dallas asked.

"Look, Rombeck," the doctor said. "You want to know if Dusty died of a heart attack, is that right?"

"Your Honor," Dallas Rombeck said, "if

it pleases the court, I would like to question the witness and not have the witness question me."

"Proceed, Mr. Rombeck," the presiding judge said.

Another half-hour. "And so," Dallas Rombeck was saying, "how can we possibly charge my client as an accomplice to a crime when we have proven conclusively that no crime was committed? The deceased, J. P. Tremaine, you have heard on medical authority, died of natural causes, induced, we submit, by the excitement of the incident at Stinson Crossing. There were, without doubt, gunshots fired. But these gunshots were fired by a person or persons unknown. I personally was there. So was my good friend Mr. Norton, the very able attorney for Mr. Donnelly. Neither Mr. Norton nor myself can truthfully say how many gunshots were fired, and Mr. Donnelly himself admits that he fired some of them—"

"I didn't figure they'd find against Tuna," Judge Norton said behind his hand.

"I don't give a damn," Hamp Donnelly said. "A court could never settle anything with Tuna."

The Judge took a watch from his vest pocket and glanced at it. "I hope we have time for your hearing this afternoon," he said.

"It won't take long," Hamp Donnelly said.

"Damn you," Judge Norton said. "Quit being so confident."

The presiding judge from The Dalles had heard at least a dozen cases similar to Hamp Donnelly's case. He half dozed through the lengthy testimony of his old friend Judge Norton. He listened to the witnesses.

It was an old fight between Orvie Stinson and Hamp Donnelly. There were a dozen character witnesses for Hamp, none for Orvie Stinson. There had been trouble before, and it was the kind of trouble that would lead to gunplay. In the mind of the presiding judge there was only one thing that needed establishing here, and that was, who fired the first shot? The presiding judge knew all the fine points of law, but in a country like this sometimes the fine points didn't count. It was a gun fight, not a murder. The magistrate leaned forward and folded his hands while Clete, the bartender from the Elkhorn, gave his testimony.

"Orvie Stinson was waiting at my saloon when I opened that morning," Clete said. "He had a .30-.30 rifle with him. He was drunk when I first seen him and he drank near a quart of whiskey at my place. He kept saying he was gonna get Hamp Donnelly.'

"Just a moment," the presiding judge said. "Are you sure those are the exact words of the deceased Orvie Stinson?"

"Orvie Stinson said he was gonna wait right there and get the dirty son of— " The bartender glanced out at the crowded courtroom. He blushed. "Orvie said he was gonna get Hamp Donnelly."

It was four-thirty in the afternoon when the visiting judge handed down his decision. There was no charge against either Tuna Stinson or Hamp Donnelly. Dallas Rombeck got up from his chair. He came over to Hamp and offered his hand. Hamp looked at the hand, then turned to Judge Norton and said, "You're a pretty good lawyer, Judge. I reckon I'll have to keep you on steady." Hamp got up, put on his hat, and walked out of the courtroom a free man. Outside the sun was hot on the dust of the street. A crowd headed for the Elkhorn, Clete hurrying ahead to unlock the door.

Hamp looked for Sue and didn't see her.

Over in front of Dallas Rombeck's law office he saw Dallas and Boyd Novis talking
to Tuna Stinson. Ned Crockett came by
and nudged Hamp with his elbow. "Sorry
to lose you as a customer, Hamp," he said.

Hamp was staring straight at Tuna Stinson. "Maybe I'll be back," he said.

"Why don't you use your head, Hamp?"
Ned Crockett said. "Why don't you forget
it?"

Hamp looked steadily at the young marshal. "Put yourself in my boots and answer
your own question, Ned," he said.

Ned Crockett looked at his friend a long
time. "Don't wear a gun in town then," the
marshal said finally. "It's against the law.
I've got yours over at the office. I'll bring
it out to the ranch in a day or so. I'm warning Tuna to stay out of town."

"You don't have to do that for me, Ned,"
Hamp said.

"I'm not doing it for you, Hamp," Ned
said quietly. "I'm doing it because it's my
job." The marshal went on up the street and
joined Dallas Rombeck, Tuna Stinson, and
Boyd Novis.

Boyd Novis looked like a weasel, Ned
Crockett thought. A thin little man with

blue-black jowls, prominent yellow teeth, and beady black eyes. Like a weasel, he was a lot of potential trouble packed in a small package. "You sounded pretty good there in court, Rombeck," Boyd Novis was saying. "I got a lot of legal stuff comes up in my business. Maybe I could use a smart young lawyer like you."

"My services are certainly available, Mr. Novis," Dallas Rombeck said, obviously flattered, "any time I can be of help to you."

"This ain't over," Tuna Stinson said. "I'll get Hamp Donnelly if it's the last thing I ever do."

"Stinson," Boyd Novis said, smiling, "you haven't got good sense. You talk too much and you use a club where kid gloves might be better. A man shouldn't use a club except as a last resort."

"You can't talk to me that way, Novis," Stinson said.

"You owe me money, Tuna," Boyd Novis said. "That gives me the right to talk any way I please."

"Get out of town, Tuna," Ned Crockett said, coming up on them.

"This is a free country," Tuna Stinson said belligerently.

"Not for you," Ned Crockett said. "Get out of town."

The veins were cords on Tuna Stinson's forehead. Boyd Novis was still smiling. "You heard the marshal, Tuna," he said. "Get out of town." The little sheepman reached into his pocket and took a twenty-dollar bill from his wallet. "Here's twenty more you owe me, Tuna," he said. "Take yourself a little trip. It strikes me you need a vacation." The sheepman turned his back on Ned Crockett and took Dallas Rombeck's arm. "And now, Mr. Rombeck," he said, "if you'd care to step into your office I'd like to talk a little business with you. Mr. Stinson here has offered to sell me his place. I don't believe we'll need him for the transaction. I already have his signature."

Ned Crockett watched the door close behind Boyd Novis and Dallas Rombeck. Ned could enforce the law, he knew, up to a point. After that there was little he could do. He turned and saw Hamp and Sue Donnelly coming up the walk toward him. Hamp had Sue's arm and he was grinning down at her. Hamp looked up and saw Ned Crockett. "Come on, Ned," he said. "I'll buy you and Sue

a dish of ice cream. I feel like cele-
brating."

—————————————————————10

Generally, transient help moved up through central Oregon at this time of year. They started in the southern part of the state, cutting hay on shares, and they moved north, nomadic people who either owned small places over on the coast or owned nothing at all. They always reminded Hamp Donnelly of his own father.

This year help was scarce. Hamp Donnelly saw the ripening meadow hay and worried about it. It was time for Ellen and Paul Tremaine to arrive and take over the ownership of Anchor, and Hamp had wanted everything to be in perfect shape for them.

A small patch five acres in extent had been mowed in the lower end of the valley. The cut hay was still there on the ground. Judge Norton had hired four men who had worked one day and quit. Now those men were across the river herding sheep for Boyd Novis on the old Stinson place. Boyd Novis had lost no time in buying up the Stinson property as soon as the trial was over. It had happened so smoothly and so quickly that there was no longer any doubt that Boyd Novis had owned the property right along. Dallas Rombeck had handled the entire transaction.

Dallas and Sue had reached a sharp disagreement over Dallas's new association with Boyd Novis, Hamp knew. Sue was worried about it. She had talked to Hamp about it, trying to defend Dallas, but her worry had shown through. It was a fine opportunity for Dallas, Hamp supposed. Boyd Novis had plenty of money—there was no doubt about that—and in his constant efforts to secure more land for his ever-increasing bands of sheep he certainly ran into situations where he could use legal counsel. Hamp Donnelly shook his head. He couldn't understand a business where a man had to cater to someone like Boyd Novis just to make a living.

It was early afternoon now and Hamp was out at the corral hitching up the team to the buckboard. He was freshly shaved and he had put on clean jeans and his best shirt. He finished hitching the team and he looked up and saw Judge Norton standing there grinning at him. "Pretty gussied up, aren't you, Hamp?" the Judge said.

"I shaved," Hamp said. "Been shaving for some time now."

"If I didn't know better," the Judge said, grinning, "I'd swear you did it for Ellen's benefit."

"Well, you know better," Hamp said gruffly. "So forget it."

The Judge was wearing his black broadcloth suit, rusty with age. A heavy gold chain was draped across the front of his vest. He took out his watch and looked at it. "We better get going if we want to meet that stage."

"Nothing holding us up, is there?" Hamp said.

"I'm sorry about the hay crew I hired," the Judge said seriously. "They looked all right to me and I figured they'd stick."

"They would have," Hamp said, "if Boyd Novis hadn't offered them more money."

The two men drove toward town, saying little, and as they crossed the shoulder of the butte both of them were thinking of Dusty Tremaine's grave up there, just where Dusty had always wanted it. Ned Crockett had let Hamp out of jail the day of the funeral. Hamp would always be grateful to Ned for that.

127

Hamp reined up at the top of the hill to let the horses blow. For a moment he looked back at the ranch and then down toward the town of Antelope. The Judge saw the worry in the younger man's eyes.

"Maybe we ought to lay all the cards out on the table, Hamp," Judge Norton said.

Hamp shook his head. "Dusty wanted Ellen and Paul to have Anchor," he said. "That's the way it's going to be." He cracked the lines against the backs of the bays, and they drove down the winding road toward Antelope at a fast trot. Hamp felt a growing excitement he couldn't name as they neared the town.

The stage was on time, marking this as a special day. Hamp Donnelly stood there waiting, and his hands were sweaty and then cold and the open collar of his shirt choked him. His memory of Ellen Tremaine waving good-by two months previous was amazingly vivid, and he stood there, tall enough to peer above the heads of the others, anxious to get a first glimpse of Ellen He had nearly forgotten that Paul, whom he had never met, would be with her. Hamp hadn't even considered the fact that Paul Tremaine would be his boss.

A dust cloud rolled up behind the careening stage, passed it, and smothered the street. Hamp started toward the stage and he saw Dallas Rombeck already there, wrenching open the door. "Ellen!" he heard Dallas shout. "Welcome back to Antelope!"

"Mr. Rombeck!" Ellen was saying. Hamp found that he had remembered the exact timbre of her voice too. "How nice of you to meet us. This is my brother Paul."

Judge Norton had managed to get up close to the stage, and now a half dozen of the town women were pressing forward and Hamp found himself on the outside of the crowd, standing alone with Sue. "Why didn't you get up close where you could say hello to Ellen?" Hamp said to his sister.

"Why didn't you?" Sue Donnelly said. She was watching Dallas and Ellen, and they were laughing and talking together and mentioning names neither Sue nor Hamp had ever heard before. Names of mutual friends back in that other world of Philadelphia.

"I didn't get in there because I don't like crowds," Hamp said.

"Neither do I," Sue said. She bit her lip. "Is three a crowd in Philadelphia, Hamp?"

"What?"

"Never mind," Sue said. "Just forget I said it."

Hamp was watching the man who stood there smiling beside Ellen Tremaine. Paul Tremaine was not very tall—about five feet eight, Hamp judged. His clothes were well made and their quality was apparent even through the wrinkles and dust of travel. Paul's age was thirty, Hamp remembered. He looked older. There was excess fat around his middle. His face was bloated and there were puffs of flesh under his eyes, a touch of gray at his temples. Hamp didn't like the color of the man's skin. It was nearly gray.

The most attractive thing about Paul Tremaine was his eyes. They were large and brown and extremely expressive. He was acknowledging introductions with casual ease, smiling. His voice was soft and resonant. "It's a pleasure meeting you, Mr. Rombeck," Paul Tremaine said. "My sister has told me all about you." He winked at Dallas Rombeck. "And so did Lucy Bannister back home," he said.

Dallas clapped a hand to his forehead in mock distress. "Oh no! Not dear Lucy!"

Voices blended in a babble of sound, and the driver and Perkins, the stage agent, were unloading hatboxes and suitcases and a steamer trunk. Paul Tremaine took a coin from his pocket and handed it to Perkins. Perkins turned the coin over in his hand, a puzzled frown between his eyes. "What's this for, Mr. Tremaine?" Perkins said.

"Here," Dallas said quickly. He took the coin and Perkins walked off scratching his head. Dallas said something behind his hand and Paul Tremaine's eyes widened. Paul shrugged his shoulders and dropped the coin back in his pocket.

Ellen Tremaine looked through the crowd and saw Hamp, and Hamp could have sworn he saw what he wanted to see in her eyes. She came toward him, smiling. "There you are, Mr. Donnelly. And Sue!" Ellen offered her hand and Hamp took it awkwardly. She put her arm around Sue.

Ellen was dressed fittingly in a gray traveling dress, and as Hamp looked at her he was acutely conscious of her nearness. Ellen's bonnet was secured in place by a velvet ribbon that passed under her chin. The black ribbon was a sharp contrast against the creamy richness of her complexion. "I know how very close you and your brother were to my uncle," Ellen said to Sue. "I want you to know it is a great comfort to me, having you here." She turned and called over her shoulder, "Paul!"

Paul Tremaine moved over to join them. He gave Sue a casual and open appraisal and then he offered his hand to Hamp. "This is Donnelly, I presume?" Paul said. "I understand we're indebted to you, Donnelly. Glad to know you."

Hamp took the hand. It was soft and moist.

Judge Norton was bustling around busily. "I'll drive Ellen out if you want, Hamp," the Judge said. "I thought maybe Sue could go along with us and sort of help Ellen get things settled."

"All right, Sue?" Hamp asked.

"Of course," Sue said. She took Ellen's arm. "You must be tired, Ellen. We could go over to the hotel and freshen up.

The two girls crossed the street together, and the townspeople stood there watching them, talking about them. Hamp found himself alone with Paul Tremaine. Hamp was ill at ease and he knew Paul was feeling the same way. "Well, I guess we're here," Paul said finally.

"It's a big country," Hamp said. "I hope you like it."

"It's a little different from what I expected," Paul said. "I haven't seen an Indian or a buffalo yet."

"We keep 'em penned up on stage day," Hamp said, grinning.

There was another long silence between the two men. Paul Tremaine glanced up the street and saw the sign of the Elkhorn Saloon. "I say, Donnelly," he said. "It was pretty dusty inside that coach. Would you care to have a drink with me to sort of launch this new venture?"

Hamp grinned. "I don't know of a better way to get acquainted," he said.

"Well, now, Donnelly," Paul Tremaine said, "I can see where we'll get along."

Hamp introduced Paul to the several men in the saloon. Clete, the bartender, mopped the bar top and smiled a merchant's welcome to a new customer. "Glad to have you with us, Mr. Tremaine," he said. "The first one's on the house. What'll it be?"

"Rye," Paul said. "I'll leave the brand up to you."

Paul downed his first drink with one gulp and sighed contentedly. "I'll swear," he said to the room in general, "I've got enough loose land in my gullet to support all the cows in Oregon."

The men all wanted to be friendly. They laughed at Paul Tremaine's humor. They all offered to buy a drink.

"Your uncle traded at my store for years, Mr. Tremaine," Jake Paxton said. "I hope that now you've taken over Anchor I can continue to have your business."

Paul Tremaine clapped the little storekeeper on the shoulder. "I really haven't much choice in the matter, have I, Jake?" he said. "It appears to me you've got the only store in town."

There was loud laughter and good fellowship, and Hamp Donnelly stood back and watched it through the gathering tobacco smoke, a small worry beginning to grow in him. Paul Tremaine was taking his drinks a little too fast and the effects were beginning to show. Either Paul wasn't used to drinking or . . . Hamp tried to put the disturbing thought out of his mind. Sometimes a man who drank too much became so saturated with the stuff that just a couple of drinks would set him off.

"I'll tell you what I'll do, Clete," Paul Tremaine said, leaning across the bar. His face was flushed and he was having trouble with his tongue. "I'll toss you a coin," he said. "Drinks for the house, double or nothing."

Clete was getting a little weary, but you had to accommodate a customer. "Sure thing, Mr. Tremaine," he said. He tossed a coin. Paul called for heads. It came tails.

Paul Tremaine laughed, but there was nervousness in his laughter. "Looks like I buy," he said. He watched Clete mix drinks for the house and then Paul reached into his pocket, and by the expression on his face Hamp knew what was coming. Paul didn't have any money.

Before Paul could say anything Hamp laid a ten-dollar bill on the bar. "What?" Paul said, glancing up quickly. "Oh no, Donnelly. This is my round." He took twenty or thirty cents out of his pocket and glanced at it. Then from his inside coat pocket he took a wallet, opened it, and thumbed through it rapidly. "Well, I'll be darned," Paul said, too much surprise in his voice. "I do believe I gave that sister of mine all my money. Say, I'll just borrow this, Donnelly. Give it back to you when we get out to the house."

"Sure," Hamp said. "Could happen to anyone."

Paul paid for the drinks with Hamp's bill and kept the change.

Hamp watched Paul's disposition change

rapidly with each drink. From exuberance to moodiness and then to surliness. One by one the others left the saloon. It was getting dark outside, and Hamp hadn't made arrangements for a rig yet. "I guess we better be getting home, Paul," Hamp said.

"You trying to tell me what to do, Donnelly?" Paul Tremaine said.

Hamp felt a touch of anger and he held it down. "Nope," be said. "Getting late, that's all. Quite a ride out to the place."

"Because if you're trying to tell me what to do, Donnelly," Paul said thickly, "just don't forget that I'm the boss and you're the hired hand. Just because I have a couple of drinks with you"—he laughed—"don't get the idea I'm just a greenhorn who don't know what he's doing."

Hamp reached out, and his fingers tightened around Paul Tremaine's arm. Clete, the bartender, saw it and turned his back on the two men. Clete knew his business. "We'll rent a rig down at the stable," Hamp said. "So long, Clete. We'll see you." The fingers tightened their grip. He felt Tremaine pull against him and then Hamp was looking deep into Paul's eyes, warning him. Paul Tremaine shrugged his shoulders.

"Be seeing you, Clete old boy," Paul said.

Hamp had to half support the man to keep him from weaving. "I'm hungry as a she-wolf with pups," Hamp said. "How does a steak sound?"

"Moo," Paul said.

"What's that?" Hamp said.

"That's the way a steak sounds," Paul said, pleased with his own brilliance. "A steak comes from a cow. A cow goes 'moo.' You see, Donnelly," he said, getting around in front of Hamp and punching Hamp's chest with a wobbly finger. "You didn't know I knew so much about the cow business, did you?" He threw back his head and opened his mouth wide. "Moooo!"

Hamp Donnelly led Paul Tremaine into the restaurant. He ordered steak rare and he ordered black coffee. Hamp sat there watching Paul Tremaine, thinking of Dusty and of Anchor. Hamp had never had any trouble with his appetite in his life. He could always eat, and food always tasted good. Now he looked at Paul Tremaine and he was thinking of Ellen and of the days ahead. He had no appetite and the steak tasted like so much wet paper.

11

Those first three weeks on Anchor Ranch were always to remain a nightmare to Ellen Tremaine. From the first time she had looked down from the shoulder of the butte to see the little house standing there, empty and alone, the full realization of her responsibility here had become a constant weight which wouldn't leave her.

When she had received the telegram from Judge Norton saying that Dusty Tremaine was dead she had felt a sadness and an emptiness which could not actually be called grief. She had grown very fond of her uncle in the month she had spent here on the ranch, but still he was nearly a stranger. He was a man who was much different from her own father and Paul, a man who had moved quietly in and out of her life for as long back as she could remember. Now as she looked at the house, the hard-packed yard, and the barrenness of the land, the death of Dusty Tremaine became real.

She was grateful for Sue Donnelly, but Sue became a stranger before she ever became a friend. Ellen had so little in common with Sue and it was almost as if Sue resented her, although Ellen couldn't decide why. Judge Norton was kind. He was always around, she could always turn to him, but in many ways Judge Norton was as remote to her as Hamp Donnelly had become. At first she had felt such a strong attraction to Hamp that it had worried her. She hadn't wanted to. She couldn't help it. Now that, too, was gone, and perhaps the loss of her feeling for Hamp was the greatest loss of all. But she still had to depend on Hamp, knowing he was the one man who would always be present and always know what to do.

The change in her feeling toward Hamp had upset her more than she cared to admit, and now she tried not to think of him as a man who had aroused a startling and disturbing emotion in her. She tried to think of him as part of the corral where the horses stirred choking dust. He was the cattle grazing on the hill. He was the butte behind the house, the butte that threw its long shadow across the ranch in the late afternoon.

It seemed to Ellen that everything had started wrong and would remain wrong. That first night when Paul had come home obviously drunk she had wanted to repack her things and walk out on Anchor Ranch and Oregon forever. Looking at Paul, she had hated Hamp Donnelly for letting her brother have a drink. The feeling had passed swiftly to be replaced by a stronger feeling. It was ridiculous to blame anyone for Paul's drinking. That night she had wished that Hamp Donnelly would put his arm around her and hold her and let her tell him all her troubles. For one second she belonged to Hamp Donnelly. She was completely and helplessly his, just for the asking. The thought had frightened her, and for days after she avoided Hamp completely.

She was dressing now, brushing her copper hair with long, swift strokes, watching herself in the mirror. Those annoying freckles had appeared again across the bridge of her nose. She detested them. The green eyes that looked back at her from the mirror were serious and worried.

She bit her lips and moistened them, bringing an attractive color. She stood up, a tall girl, long-limbed, beautifully formed. She was attractive, she knew, and as she stepped into her new divided riding skirt she thought of Dallas Rombeck, who had promised to take her riding today. She brushed her hair back and tied it at the nape of her neck with a green ribbon and she felt a normal girl's pleasure at knowing she looked just right. The one bright spot in her life these days was Dallas Rombeck. And Dallas Rombeck was the man who had told her the one thing that had turned her so completely against Hamp Donnelly, making her fear the man.

She threw the brush down on the bureau top and tried to put the disturbing thought out of her mind, but it wouldn't go away. Sometimes she awoke at night thinking about it. Thinking of Hamp Donnelly, this strange, silent man who had awakened unbidden emotions in her. This man who was part of Anchor and therefore part of her life. She tried to picture the man she knew standing with a gun in his hand, deliberately, plannedly, killing another man. A small shudder ran through her frame. She hurried out of the house, wanting to be in the open and in the sunlight.

Hamp Donnelly was out at the corral. She saw him patiently examining the forefoot of one of the horses and she remembered the kindness she had sensed in the man. He was quiet, always pleasant, tremendously efficient. Efficient at killing a man, too, she thought. Tracking a man down the way an animal would track prey.

141

Tracking and killing. There was a quiet revulsion in her as she walked, thinking back
to that day when Hamp had fought with
Orvie Stinson.

She could remember Orvie Stinson viv-
idly. Big, hulking, ugly. And yet at this
moment her sympathy was all with the
sheepman. Orvie Stinson was dead; Hamp
Donnelly had killed him. She had seen these
two men fight with their fists, sensed the
animal hatred between them. Hamp Donnelly had whipped Orvie Stinson that day,
but that, obviously, hadn't been enough for
this quiet blue-eyed man who ate at the
same table with Ellen Tremaine. His anger
whetted, Hamp Donnelly had had to have
more. So he had tracked Orvie Stinson
down and killed him with a gun. . . .

"Morning, Miss Ellen," Hamp Donnelly
said.

His voice reached out and struck at her.
She drew her breath in sharply, turned and
walked rapidly away. She found she was
gripping her hands until the nails bit into
the palms.

It was only a short wait before Dallas
Rombeck arrived, and she was glad of that.
It seemed to Hamp, watching them, that
Ellen was overly pleased with seeing Dallas

and he felt a small annoyance. It was just that he didn't want Dallas to become too familiar with the workings of Anchor, Hamp kept telling himself, but he knew secretly that it was more than that. Hamp hadn't missed Ellen's original interest in him. It had both flattered and thrilled him.

Dallas came over toward the corral. He was perfectly groomed, wearing an Ascot tie, a low-crowned flat-brimmed hat, plain, polished knee-length boots. "Ellen's horse ready, Hamp?" Dallas called.

Hamp jerked his thumb toward the animal he had saddled and spit at the toe of his boot. "Sue tells me you and Boyd Novis are hittin' it off just fine," Hamp said.

Dallas looked at Hamp quickly. "Is that supposed to mean something?"

"I just wondered how you stood the stink," Hamp said.

There was a slight flush in Dallas Rombeck's cheeks. "You can be pretty unpleasant, Hamp," he said.

"With you, yes," Hamp said.

"Why?" Dallas asked. "What have I ever done to you?"

"You talk too much, Rombeck," Hamp said, thinking of Ellen.

143

"Hamp, I've tried my best to be friendly with you," Dallas started.

"There's the horse," Hamp said. "Miss Ellen's waiting." He flipped up a stirrup and gave the cinch a final tug. He handed the reins to Rombeck. For a second the gazes of the two men locked. "Look, Rombeck," Hamp said. "If Boyd Novis has made another offer to buy Anchor why don't you just forget it? Ellen and Paul don't want to sell."

"If you don't mind, Donnelly," Dallas Rombeck said, "I'll discuss the business of Anchor with the owners, not with you." He led the horse over to where Ellen was waiting and he walked stiffly, his temper showing in the set of his shoulders. Hamp Donnelly took a match from his shirt pocket. He inserted it in his mouth and bit it in two. My future brother-in-law, Hamp thought dismally. He saw Dallas helping Ellen into the saddle, saw their hands meet and linger together too long. Or maybe you're lucky, Sue. Maybe you've lost him to Ellen, Hamp thought. He found that idea as bitter as the first.

The press of necessary work soon drove the disturbing thoughts from Hamp's mind. He had hired another haying crew and had them started, but now it was late in the season. Clouds had been piling around the snow peaks of the Cascades the last few days, and this morning, up on the hill at sunup, he hadn't been able to see Mount Hood. Hamp glanced toward the house and knew that in all probability Paul Tremaine was still in bed. Paul rarely put in an appearance before ten o'clock in the morning. To Hamp, used to using the sun for a watch, it was near sacrilege.

Hamp had hoped that Paul would gradually work into the routine of things but, if anything, it seemed as if Paul was growing farther away from it. Paul openly hated Anchor and all its surroundings and never missed an opportunity to say so. Hamp glanced at the butte, red with morning sun. I'm trying my damnedest, Dusty, he said to himself.

There was some harness to mend, a place in the corral fence to patch. Hamp had to drive into Antelope for supplies this afternoon and Ellen wanted to go with him to buy some curtains and things for the house. As Hamp had drifted off to sleep last night the thought of Ellen going to town with him had been pleasantly uppermost in his mind. Now the pleasure was gone. He hadn't missed the way she had looked at him this morning, the way she had avoided him the past couple of weeks.

At first he hadn't been able to figure out what it was, but a chance conversation at the supper table with Judge Norton one night had told him. Hamp and the Judge had been discussing guns and Hamp had reached up and taken down Dusty's old .45 that still hung loaded in its holster on the elk horns there above the table. Hamp had held Dusty's gun in his hand, his finger loosely through the trigger guard, and then he had flipped his hand and the perfect balance of the gun had dropped the weapon into his palm. At that instant Ellen Tremaine came through the kitchen door. Hamp looked at her and saw her face, dead white. He saw the same revulsion in her eyes that he had seen once in the eyes of a woman looking at her first rattlesnake. And then he knew. He had put the gun away and finished his meal in silence, knowing that whatever emotion had been growing between himself and Ellen was now dead. Dallas Rombeck must have done a fine job of telling you about my killing of Orvie Stinson, Hamp thought.

The sun was warm. He should be out

146

keeping an eye on that haying crew, Hamp knew, but a man couldn't be two places at once. He hadn't been too pleased with the looks of that crew—a man and his two sons. The old man had done all the talking, whining and complaining, trying to get more money for the job. Hamp was busy working on the fence. He didn't notice the rider coming down the road from Antelope until the man was almost in the barnyard. Hamp straightened, dropping his hammer. It was one of the sons from the haying crew and he had come from the direction of Antelope, not from the direction of the meadow where he was supposed to be working.

Hamp felt the quick anger he always felt toward anyone shirking a job. "Where the devil you been?" he said to the rider.

"In town," the man on horseback said. "Anything wrong with that?" He was an awkward-looking youth with buck teeth and a pimply face. He was riding one of the wagon horses, using a battered McClellan saddle. There were two gunny sacks tied together and slung behind the saddle.

"I hired you to cut hay, not go running off to town," Hamp said.

"Hell, man," the youth said thinly. "We

147

got to eat, don't we? Can't eat hay. I had to go get some grub."

"I stocked you up yesterday," Hamp said. "What happened to that?"

The kid leaned forward and there was a wide smirk on his face. "Don't go gettin' so uppity with me, Donnelly," he said. "Your job ain't the only job in Oregon. Fact is, me and Paw and Brother Lonnie talked it over and we decided you ain't payin' us enough."

"From the looks of it," Hamp said, "I'm payin' you ten times what you're worth." He fought down his temper, realizing he had to have this help. That was one thing he hated about haying time. It made him dependent on outside help. "All right," Hamp said. "But I hope you bought enough grub to last you a few days."

"If I ain't," the youth said, "I can always go get more." He nudged the wide-belly horse in the ribs and rode on toward the trail that led to the meadows, riding with a deliberate slowness.

Hamp picked up the hammer and his hand gripped the handle. He stood there looking after the youth and he gritted his teeth and drew the hammer back in a striking motion. He let the breath run out of his lungs and went back to repairing the fence.

Two hours later Hamp had the team harnessed and was waiting for Ellen to get back so he could drive her into town. He stood there leaning against the wheel of the light spring wagon, smoking a cigarette, gazing toward the crest of the low hill that stood between the hay meadows and the house. It was still early, but the three-man hay crew had quit work and now they were coming up the trail on foot. The cigarette smoke turned brassy in Hamp's mouth. There was no doubt in his mind what those men wanted.

Hamp let the father of the two boys do the talking. "I'm an honorable man," the old man said. "When I give my word it's my bond, but a man has to eat. Now if you could up our pay and furnish all the grub to boot—"

"I made a deal with you," Hamp Donnelly said, fighting to control himself. "You accepted it."

"Shucks now, Donnelly," the old man said, sure of himself. "You can't blame a feller none if he's got a chance to make a sight more money for less work."

"Herding sheep for Boyd Novis, maybe?" Hamp said.

"I reckon I ain't free to divulge that," the old man said.

At that moment Dallas Rombeck and Ellen Tremaine came riding into the yard at a fast canter. Ellen's hair was blowing loose and she was laughing, shouting back at Dallas. They had apparently had a race and Ellen had won it. They slid their horses to a stop, and Hamp saw the laughter run out of Ellen's eyes as she saw the three men standing there. "What is it, Hamp?" she asked.

"It's all right, Miss Ellen," Hamp said. "I'll handle it."

"Maybe I ought to put the proposition to the boss there," the old man said.

Ellen Tremaine slipped out of the saddle easily and came and stood beside Hamp. "What is it?" she repeated.

The old man took off his hat and scratched his muddy gray hair. "Like I was telling your foreman here, miss," he said. "Me and my boys, Lonnie and Newt, figger you jest ain't payin' us enough."

"Are you paying them the figure they agreed on?" Ellen said.

"That's right," Hamp said. "They got an offer of more money."

Hamp saw the quick anger flare into Ellen Tremaine's eyes and he saw the tilt of her chin. It reminded him of Dusty. "You listen to me," Ellen said to the three men. She had put her hands on her hips and taken a step closer to them. "You made an agreement with us to cut that hay for so much. If you think you can loaf two days and then come in here and hold us up you've got another think coming. Either get back there and get to work on that hay at the price we agreed on or come on over to the house and draw your pay, and I don't care which. I'm getting sick and tired of a shiftless bunch of—of—of tramps like you three thinking you can take advantage of me just because I'm a woman. You've been piddling around down there for two days now, and I could have cut more hay by myself. You're not worth half of what we're payin' you and you have the gall to stand there and whine for more money. You and those two big louts!" She stamped her foot. "Figure out what we owe them, Hamp, and send them over to the house. I wouldn't have this trash on my ranch for five minutes!"

Ellen turned and walked swiftly toward the house, her heels pounding against the hard ground. "Whew!" the old man said.

"She ain't got that red hair for nothin', has she?"

Hamp Donnelly was grinning broadly and he felt as if he were about to burst wide open. "She ain't got the name Tremaine for nothing," Hamp said.

"What's that?" the old man said.

"I said you heard the boss," Hamp said. "Go draw your pay and get the hell out of here before she really loses her temper and throws you out."

A moment later Hamp saw Ellen on the front porch handing the three men a check and he knew she was giving them a second tongue lacing hotter than the first. Hamp Donnelly wanted to jump in the air and yell. He felt if he didn't the pride inside him would surely choke him. There was a Tremaine, that Ellen. She was all Tremaine.

Paul came out of the house at that moment and went over and joined Dallas. The two men sat down on a bench in the shade of the wind-break poplars and talked together. In a little while Ellen came out to the wagon. She had taken time to change her clothes, but she was still fighting mad. "I didn't know if you'd still want to go to town or not," Hamp said.

"Of course I do," she said hotly. "Why shouldn't I?"

"Well, I figgered maybe—"

"Well, just 'unfigger' it, whatever it was," she said. She climbed into the seat of the wagon before he could help her. Hamp Donnelly whistled a small tune, and a larger tune sang inside him. He climbed into the seat, unwrapped the lines, and drove toward town.

The anger ran slowly out of Ellen Tremaine. She knew tears were close and she fought them back. That haying crew trying to hold her up for more money had been the final straw. It had seemed to her in that moment that everything in this country was trying to work against her. She had let her temper go and she was glad that she had.

The grind of the wagon wheels grated against her nerves. The road lifted and the land lay there below her. It was wide and lonely, foreboding and unfriendly. The reaction of her anger came and brought with it a tremendous let-down and a terrific loneliness. She wished suddenly it were Dallas Rombeck driving her to town instead of Hamp Donnelly. She glanced at Hamp.

His eyes were crinkled tightly against the glare and he was grinning widely. His jaw was blocky and square, his cheekbones high, pulling the bronze skin tight across his face. He was strikingly handsome at the moment and she hated him for it. He looked like the cat that swallowed the rat. You just loved my getting mad, didn't you, Hamp Donnelly? she thought to herself. You thrive on trouble.

All the loneliness and the strangeness of the land were there. All the worry over Paul. The countless things she couldn't understand. And above all, though she fought against it, was the realization that she had started to fall in love with a killer. This man who was sitting no more than six inches away from her was a man who had killed another man with a gun. A sob caught in her throat, and without realizing she was doing it she moved a little farther to her side of the seat. The tears were begging for release and her chest was burning. I can't stand much more of this, she said to herself. I can't stand much more. . . .

They came down toward the town, and a single rider was there ahead of them in the road, a huge, hulking man who rode slouched. There was a blanket roll behind

154

his saddle. The man's clothes were covered with fine dust and the horse was sweaty, as if they had come a long way.

Ellen watched the rider and there was something vaguely familiar about him, but she couldn't tell just what it was.

Immediately she sensed a change in Hamp Donnelly. She glanced at him. The grin was gone. Hamp's lips were so tight they pulled away from his teeth. His shoulders were tense and she saw that the knuckles of his hands were white from gripping the lines. She saw his eyes then, wickedly bright, staring at that solitary rider going down the road ahead of them.

They drove past the schoolhouse. Two boys were standing in the yard and they, too, were staring at the rider. She saw one of the boys wave timidly. The man on horseback didn't look around.

A wild fear started growing in Ellen Tremaine. She didn't know why. It was as if a wave of feeling were coming from Hamp Donnelly, passing through her own body. It was as if something evil were emanating from Hamp, reaching out and touching her. She glanced at Hamp Donnelly's eyes and then had to turn and look away. She couldn't bear what she saw there. A killer's eyes, she thought to herself. It was impossible to make that thought go away.

12

Two women joined the little group around Ellen Tremaine there in front of Jake Paxton's store, and as Hamp Donnelly passed them he heard Ellen talking with that peculiar rush of words that marks a woman starved for conversation. He glanced at her and saw that she could still smile and he was glad. He went inside the store and the storekeeper turned his head and spit at his handy coffee can. "Some looker, ain't she?"

"Miss Ellen?" Hamp said.

"Kinda picky, though. She'll have to get used to the fact that Antelope ain't Philadelphia. Asked fer stuff I never heerd of."

"Start totin' it out," Hamp said. "I gotta get loaded."

The storekeeper wiggled his body as if he were trying to dig his elbows into the counter. "What you gonna do, Hamp, the hay crew quittin' on Miss Ellen that way? How you gonna get your hay cut?"

"I'll bite it off with my teeth," Hamp said. He picked up a bolt of material that Ellen

Tremaine had chosen for curtains. "Wrap something around this."

The storekeeper's faded eyes were sharp behind his glasses. "You reckon the hay crew quit because they figgered there'd be more trouble?"

"Are you asking questions, Jake, or running a store?"

"Hell, Hamp," the storekeeper said. "No call for you to get sore at me."

He was talking to empty space. Hamp Donnelly had picked up a box of groceries and now he was outside, loading it into the wagon. He glanced down the street to where the trail-sweaty horse was tied in front of the Elkhorn Saloon and he knew Tuna Stinson was inside. Tuna was inside getting drunk, making his brag, waiting for Hamp to start it. . . . Hamp turned back to enter the store, and Ned Crockett was there, blocking his way. "You stay away from Tuna, Hamp," the marshal said.

"Tell him the same then, Ned," Hamp said. He went back into the store. The marshal turned and walked quickly down the street past the women and he lifted his hat to them. Hamp saw Ned turn in at the hotel and go up the covered stairway on the outside.

The storekeeper kept twisting and digging his elbows into the counter. He had a tic in his left eye. "Hamp, what kinda feller's Miss Ellen's brother?" he asked. "I only seen him that first day when they come in on the stage from The Dalles. Is the brother anything like their uncle was? I hear tell the brother and Dallas Rombeck is thick as fleas."

"You hear a hell of a lot, don't you, Jake?" Hamp said. He picked up a hundred-pound sack of sugar and tossed it across his shoulder. "Make sure you got a spud stuck on the spout of that coal-oil can," he said. "I don't want it leaking all over this sugar."

Hamp finished loading the wagon and from time to time he glanced down toward the saloon, the feeling of suppressed anger strong in him. Tuna Stinson's horse was still there. That was like Tuna. He would spend his first day in town getting drunk, building up his anger and whetting his hatred. Hamp wished he could start it now, get it over. He remembered the way Ellen had looked at him. He passed a rope around a hook on the wagon bed and secured it over the top of the tarp. His hands were heavy and square from work and they were bulky and big against the rope, but they were not clumsy. The marshal came out of the hotel and walked back up the street toward the wagon. He walked as if he were tired. "I just talked to Boyd Novis," the marshal said.

"Did you expect Novis to admit he sent for Tuna?" Hamp said.

"Damn it, Hamp," the marshal said. "I can only do so much."

Hamp's expression softened as he looked at the younger man. "Sure, Ned," he said. "Forget it." He walked around the wagon and stood there, his hat pushed back on his unruly blond hair. "All loaded, Miss Ellen."

She glanced at him, impatiently, he thought, but she said good-by to the women and then she came to the wagon. He helped her up, acutely aware of her nearness. His hands were strong around her waist and he lifted her easily until her foot was on the hub and she climbed into the seat hurriedly, wanting to be free of the touch of his hands. He could sense that. Damn it, Hamp thought, do you think I enjoyed killing a man any more than you enjoy thinking about it?

His hands gripped the lines with an angry strength. He kicked off the brake and tooled the Anchor-branded team of matched bays away from the store porch. "I want to stop by the school a minute and say hello to my sister," he said.

"Of course." Ellen was staring straight ahead, her lips tight, sitting far over on her side of the seat. He could feel her shrinking away from him. Do you want to see my hands? he thought. Do you want to see the blood on them?

They drove down the single street of the town, past the law office of Dallas Rombeck, and he noticed the office was closed. Dallas, then, was still at the ranch with Paul. Hamp slapped the lines against the backs of the bays. He wanted to forget Dallas.

Ahead, across the little valley, the hills lifted, marked by the single twisting road that led into the broken country toward Anchor Ranch and the lush valleys of the John Day River. Gradually the anger ran out of Hamp and he tried to visualize what it would be like if all this were as strange to him as it was to Ellen and Paul. But it annoyed him at times that she and her brother hadn't been better prepared for it. They had always known that someday they would inherit Anchor. The anger was gone and he felt a protective affection for Ellen. She was doing

160

all right, actually. He wanted to tell her so. The way she had handled that hay crew . . . For a second he forgot Tuna. A small grin crinkled the corners of his eyes. "That hay crew will have red ears for a week," he said.

He saw her chin come up, her lips tighten, and it pleased him. "Quit, will they?" she said. "Of all the worthless, no good trash—" Her chin was trembling a bit and she didn't try to say more. But she knew how to take trouble, Hamp decided. Maybe she would even understand how it was with Tuna Stinson. . . . He turned the team and his elbow brushed her shoulder. He felt her wince away from him as if his elbow had been a hot iron.

The schoolhouse was in a field by the road, a small one-room building with twin outhouses and a combination buggy and woodshed. It was recess time and a dozen children were playing noisily. Two boys were wrestling, rolling around in the dirt of a hard-packed yard while Sue stood near them, trying to stop them. Three pig-tailed girls clung to Sue's skirts and moved when she moved, like chicks around a mother hen. Hamp put his foot against the brake and spoke to the team as he twisted his hands against the lines. "I'll just be a minute."

"Sue is as pretty as a picture," Ellen said. She waved to Sue and to the two little boys who had run out toward the road at breakneck speed and then stopped dead still to stand and stare.

"She takes after me," Hamp said. It didn't sound very funny. He got down from the wagon and walked across the yard, tousling the head of a ten-year-old boy who came out to meet him. Sue gave the girls near her a spat on the bottom and shooed them away before going over to join her brother. She turned and walked with him toward the pump that stood in back of the school building. Hamp pushed back his hat, placed his hand under the spout of the pump, worked the handle, and drank the dammed-up water. "How's it going, Sue?" he said.

She stood there, a small, beautifully formed girl, just out of her teens. Her eyes were a deep blue, her hair black, and he always had trouble remembering that she had grown up. "All right," Sue said. "How's the Queen?"

"Miss Ellen?" Hamp grinned. "She's all right." It was more than an answer to the question. "The hay crew quit. Ellen really gave 'em a piece of her mind."

Sue still stood there watching him. "Well, why don't you ask me about Dallas?"

Hamp shrugged. "Dallas Rombeck ain't the only man left in the world."

"Suppose I tell you he is for me?" There was an amazing amount of determination in that small body.

He crooked his finger under her chin and tried to grin. "I've never tried to make up your mind for you, Pie Face, but I won't lie and say Dallas is the one I'd pick for a brother-in-law. He's a little highfalutin for my taste."

"But not for the Queen's taste?"

"She's just lonesome, that's all. She and Dallas visit about them folks they knew back East. I reckon they talk the same language."

Sue folded her arms defiantly across her breasts. "Don't tell me she's got you seeing stars too?"

Hamp ignored the remark. "Come on out to the wagon and say hello to her."

"Do I have to?" she asked sulkily.

"Yes."

They walked together, back around the school building. The children clamored at

Hamp, calling him by his first name. There was a wild babble of voices, a dozen conversations, none of them making sense, and then one voice, young and strident, was louder than the rest. "Hamp could too lick Tuna Stinson with one hand tied behind him!"

"Yeah?" another jeered. "Did you see Tuna when he come ridin' down the road a while ago? Did you talk to him like I did?"

"You're a liar! You didn't talk to Tuna!"

Sue's face had drained of color. "When did he come back, Hamp?"

"About an hour ago."

"Why didn't you tell me?"

"For what?" Hamp said. "He's here, so he's here. We knew he'd be back sometime."

Sue's voice was trembling with emotion. "Don't fight with him, Hamp. I couldn't go through it again. Go away someplace for a little while—"

"That's crazy talk," he said flatly.

Sue's voice was bitter. "How long are you going to keep this up? Are you going to get yourself killed just so she can go on being the grand lady?"

"I guess it don't seem very grand to her," he said. He took his sister's arm. "Look,

Sue. You've lived here all your life and you can understand things like this. You knew I had to kill Orvie Stinson; you knew Tuna would come back sometime. Miss Ellen's different, Sue. I don't want her to know about Tuna being here. Not just yet."

Sue pulled away and stood there. "You're a fool, Hamp."

"Maybe," he said. "You be nice to her." He put his hand under Sue's elbow and they walked on toward the wagon.

Ellen had climbed down from the wagon and she was half kneeling, her full skirt spread around her, her arm around a dingy child who stood embarrassed, thumb in mouth. A nine-year-old boy strutted in front of her and spit across the center of his lip. Ellen put her free arm around the strutting boy and squeezed him close, and the boy dug his bare toe in the dirt and ducked his head. Ellen looked up and saw Hamp and Sue watching her and she stood up, smoothing her skirt. There was a wistful half smile in Ellen's eyes as she watched the children run back toward the schoolhouse. "Kids are all alike, aren't they?" she said.

"Very much so," Sue Donnelly said. "I'm afraid Easterners think our children out here run around naked with feathers in their hair. Actually—"

Hamp coughed against the back of his hand. "I reckon we better be moseyin' along before it gets too late."

"I wish you'd come out and see me, Sue," Ellen said. "I've missed you. I bought some curtain material and several things for the house. I'm dying to have you see them. It's really pretty difficult, though, shopping in Antelope."

"I've shopped here all my life without any trouble," Sue said. The girl who was monitor started dinging the teacher's desk bell and children ran from every direction. "If you'll excuse me—" Sue turned quickly and walked over to the school steps and stood there clapping her hands together, calling to the children. Hamp Donnelly saw the smile fade slowly from Ellen Tremaine's face.

13

Hamp stopped the wagon at the top of the hill. The horses stood spread-legged, sweat dripping from their bellies, and the animal smell was strong. To Hamp it was a good,

166

clean smell. He glanced at Ellen and saw her nostrils flare. "Good look at the town down there, ain't it?" he said.

She turned and looked back and down. Antelope was below them, a square of green in a tan land. She could see the school and the roof of Paxton's store and she thought of the women she had talked to. She remembered how they often referred to "Hamp's trouble with the Stinsons." It was something she wanted to talk about and yet she could never quite bring herself to discuss it. Hamp's voice reached through to her.

"I reckon it ain't as big as Philadelphia, is it?" he said.

She tried to smile. "It's pretty small, all right."

"The big country is this way," he said.

He looked across the distance to the canyon of the John Day River, twisting and green, and beyond that were the brown hills, lonely and never ending in their sameness, dismally alike to one who didn't know them, comforting in their permanence and sameness to one who did. He glanced at her and saw the tightness of her lips, her hands gripped in her lap, her eyes straight ahead. "This was your uncle's favorite spot," he said quietly. "I'll take you to his grave up there on the butte sometime if you want.

Perhaps it was the mention of her uncle, or maybe it was only that emotions could be held just so long. She turned toward him and her eyes were bright, her lips set in a hard line. She wasn't really beautiful, he realized. She was just close to beauty. So close that a man watched her constantly, expecting each change of expression to bring perfection. She was angry now. Angry and hurt. "Why do they hate me?" she said. "What have I ever done to any of them?"

"Miss Ellen, they don't hate you. Nobody could."

"Even your sister. What have I ever done to her? That haying crew. Why did they walk out just when we needed them most?"

"You can't depend on a crew like that," he said patiently. "Next month they'll be up in the Umatilla country workin' the wheat. Maybe later they'll be down at the mouth of the Columbia canning salmon. They're just drifters."

"They were hired away from us, just like the crew before them. Boyd Novis hired them. He paid them twice what we could pay them."

"We'll get by, Miss Ellen," he said.

The entire distance between the deep canyon of the Deschutes and the winding green valleys of the John Day was there below them, a high land of gently rolling hills, sharp canyons, flats and valleys, gray with sage, brown with grass, musty green with scattered juniper. West the magnificence of Mount Hood reared unbroken snow fields above the darkness of fir forests, and to the south Mount Jefferson stood in isolated splendor, and beyond that were blue mountains and snow peaks. The colors of afternoon came out of the day and mixed themselves on the palette of endless space, and the awesome silence was everywhere. A faint odor of sage and cured grass spiced the thin, clean air with an illusive fragrance, and the reds and the golds retreated from the purple hills.

For a moment then he was close to her again. She was not afraid of him and he could say the things he had been wanting to say, let her know that she wasn't alone, that he himself cared very much what happened to her and her brother, and that Judge Norton cared just as much. . . . "You've done good for the short time you've been here, Miss Ellen," he said quietly. "You and Paul both. If Dusty's watching you from up there he's mighty proud of you."

She turned and looked at him. He was gazing off into space, and the hard lines of his face had softened and there was a dream in his eyes. Again he was a man and not a fixture she had inherited with the ranch. The illusion passed quickly and she was remembering that this man had killed—that he was as hard and ruthless as the land itself.

He glanced at her and saw the change in her expression. There was a lot he wanted to tell her, but he couldn't just yet. He couldn't tell her until she was ready to understand. He looked away. "Me and the Judge worried about you and your brother coming out here, everything new to you." He hadn't realized he would have so much trouble saying the simple thing he wanted to say. "We know now you'll make out all right, Miss Ellen. When you turned down the cash offer Boyd Novis made you we knew you liked Anchor well enough to want to keep it."

She sat there staring at him, listening to this man who had once stirred her so strongly, this man who now frightened her. She felt the land around them, barren and vast and unfriendly. A land that could kill, peopled with men who killed. A terrifying wave of loneliness swept over her and grew into a homesickness that was physical pain. She thought of her brother Paul and of how he fit this even less than she did. She spoke without even meaning to say the words aloud. "Like it?" She was looking straight at Hamp now, and all the bitterness was in her eyes. "I hate it! I hate every stone and every blade of grass and every cow and every piece of dust and every breath of air I breathe!"

The humor ran out of Hamp Donnelly's eyes. He felt as if someone had hit him in the pit of the stomach. He took his foot off the brake and drove down the hill toward the ranch in the valley and he kept thinking, over and over, Has she told you this, Dallas Rombeck? Do you know how she feels?

Hamp tooled the wagon into the hard-packed yard between the ranch house and the barn and pulled the now sweaty team to a stop. Paul Tremaine and Dallas Rombeck, talking in the house, had heard the creak of the wagon and the grind of the wheels an hour before the outfit came in sight. They were out in the yard waiting.

Ellen didn't wait for Hamp to help her down. She ran to Paul and kissed him on the cheek and gave her hand to Rombeck. The touch of Dallas's fingers was like reaching out and finding something familiar in a dark room. Ellen and Dallas and Paul always had something to say to each other. If nothing else, there were the people back home. Dallas knew people by name whom Ellen knew by name. By now those people who were only names had become close mutual friends when contrasted against her loneliness here. Things that were amusing to her were amusing to Dallas, and for this moment, at least, she could pretend. "Dallas! Paul! Wait until you see what I bought! Three kinds of curtain material and a new reflector lamp for the kitchen wall and—you'll love this, Paul—some stove blacking for Iron Dragon—" Dallas had named the kitchen stove that. She felt if she didn't keep talking she would cry.

"It must have been very gay," Paul Tremaine said. "Did you get out before they rolled the streets up?"

"Street, singular, my friend," Dallas Rombeck said. "Don't try to foist growth upon our fair city. Anything but that."

"The place gives me the creeps," Paul said. He was a handsome man in spite of his weight, and the streak of premature gray in his dark hair gave him a certain dignity. His face was fixed in the constant scowl that was so much a part of him.

"Oh, come, Paul," Rombeck said, slapping his friend on the back. "We're not all savages here, in spite of what you think."

"Dallas, what would we do without you?" Ellen said. She took both men by the arm and led them toward the substantial frame house. "Come along, you two, if you want any dinner."

"A banquet," Dallas said. "I brought you some select wine." He kissed her fingertips.

Hamp stood there and watched them go toward the house, three people totally different and yet much alike. He saw the neat cut of Dallas Rombeck's coat, the tailored shoulders and fitted waist. The brown trousers were a perfect fit, tight at the ankles, snug above the polished black boots that looked as if they had never seen dust. Successful or not, Dallas Rombeck always looked the part of the properous young attorney. There was a studied carelessness about Paul's dress, and Hamp sensed that

173

it was something that could be achieved only by a man who knew exactly how to dress. Hamp started unhitching the team, his hands moving swiftly.

The screen door of the bunkhouse opened and slammed closed and Judge Norton stood there on the step a moment, then crossed over to the corral, walking carefully, mindful of his joints. His voice was as dry and as seamed as his skin. "Did she pay 'em off?"

"She paid 'em off and told 'em oft," Hamp said. "She's got spunk, that one."

"That makes six men in all Boyd Novis has hired away from her."

"I can count," Hamp said.

"What next, Hamp?" the Judge said. "Novis is getting anxious for more graze. You can see that."

"Too anxious, maybe," Hamp said.

The Judge caught something in Hamp's voice. There was quick concern in his pin-bright eyes. "What do you mean by that?" the Judge said quickly.

"Tuna Stinson's in town."

The Judge removed his pipe from his mouth. He held it in his hand, gripping it until the bowl burned his thin flesh. "Does Ellen know?"

"About Tuna?" Hamp shrugged. He pulled the harness free and hung it on the fence. "She will. Somebody will see to that."

A light lamp flared up in the living room of the ranch house. Hamp and the Judge could hear Ellen and Dallas Rombeck laughing together. The two men stood there, one old, one young, their features growing dim in the gathering dusk. "You couldn't keep trouble away from her forever," the Judge said.

"I didn't expect to."

There was a long silence between them, and Hamp thought of the grave on the butte. He tried to think the way Dusty Tremaine would have thought. He led the horses to the trough and let them drink, hearing them swallow noisily in the gathering darkness, and then he turned them into the corral. For a moment he stood there, watching them circle and paw before lying down to roll the sweat out of their hides. He could hear the Judge breathing heavily with a dry, rasping sound, as if trying to control what he wanted to say, weighing and testing each word before he said it. "Maybe it's no good, Hamp," he said finally. "Maybe it's not worth it.

"Dusty wanted them to stay, didn't he?" Hamp said.

From inside the house he could hear Ellen's laughter. He stood there a moment, listening, and he remembered a time when he and Sue were small and Sue had refused to go to a birthday party because she didn't like some of the little girls who were going to be there. Sue's and Hamp's father had told her if she didn't go and have a good time she'd get the licking of her life. Sue went; she had a good time; she laughed and played harder than anyone and all the time she was thinking about getting that licking. Ellen Tremaine's laughter made Hamp think of that. "We better get washed up for supper," Hamp said.

"She didn't ask me for supper," the Judge said. "Maybe I better not come."

"Since when do you have to be asked to eat at Dusty Tremaine's table?" Hamp asked.

They went over to the kitchen door where the bucket and tin basin sat on a water- and soap-soaked bench. Inside, busy in the kitchen, Ellen could hear them washing and she could hear that peculiar, burbling sound the Judge always made when he washed his face. She was slightly

176

annoyed that the Judge was going to stay. She wished just she and Paul and Dallas could have eaten alone.

She could hear Dallas and Paul talking in the dining room and she went to the door and looked in, giving Dallas her quick smile. Paul was pacing back and forth across the room, his hands thrust deep into his trouser pockets, the eternal scowl on his face. The crystal wine decanter which she had brought with her from Philadelphia was there on the table, two-thirds empty now.

Dallas looked up and saw her and returned her smile. "Isn't there something I can do to help you?" She was suddenly aware of his handsomeness. He was always pleasant, always completely at ease. It was comforting to have him around.

"You can set the table," she said, and she held the door open for him. His shoulder brushed hers as he came into the kitchen.

She pushed a strand of hair off her forehead with her wrist and pointed to the cupboard with a spatula. "If you can find five plates to match," she said, "we'll make this dinner formal."

"Five?"

"Judge Norton is staying."

"He practically lives here, doesn't he?"

She didn't answer. Hamp and the Judge came in through the back door. There was fifty years' difference in their ages, a foot difference in their height, and yet they looked alike, somehow, just as she had found most men did in this country. Their faces were scrubbed, their hair combed in that peculiar fashion that made it look as if it would stay in place exactly for the duration of the meal, no longer. They passed through the kitchen, hats in hand, and they hung their hats on the elk antlers in the dining room, where Dusty Tremaine's old single-action .45 hung in its holster, loaded, just as he had left it. Ellen had intended a dozen times to put that gun away, but she didn't like the thought of handling it.

Rombeck nodded to Hamp and the Judge and gave his attention to Ellen. "The silver candelabra, perhaps, madame? And the crystal service?"

"The cups with handles," she said, "and be thankful."

Hamp and the Judge pulled out their chairs and sat down, and now they were waiting there, wondering what to to do with their hands Hamp never seemed to be entirely at ease unless he was outside.

"How about a glass of wine?" Ellen heard Paul say. She thought Paul's voice was a little loud and she hurried with the meal.

————————————————————11

The food was good; the candles Ellen had on the table gave a small, festive glow she liked, though she had the feeling Hamp and the Judge were searching for their food in the semi-darkness. Rombeck's conversation was as pleasant as usual, and even the Judge seemed to be trying hard tonight, but the meal was spoiled because of Paul.

Paul had had too much wine and instead of cheering him it had driven him farther into his morose shell. His dark eyes were bright, his lips too red against the pallor of his skin. He put down his knife and fork, too hard. "Gravy," he said. "Fried meat. Fried potatoes. What I'd give for a dozen oysters on the half shell."

"First time you get over to Portland there's a restaurant there famous for oysters, I hear," Hamp said. "Never tried 'em myself."

"Speaking of oysters," Dallas Rombeck said, "remember that little place just off Market in Philadelphia? You went downstairs." He touched his lips with his napkin. "I remember one night several of us—James Pitkin was along. Ellen, you remember James Pitkin—"

She was really interested in what Dallas had to say. It made her homesick in the comforting way a visitor from home makes one homesick. She wanted to listen but she couldn't. She was watching Paul, worried now. "Where'd you say this burgundy comes from, Dallas?" Paul asked. He had taken the stopper from the wine decanter and dropped it. He poured his glass full.

"Santa Rosa, down in California, in the Sonoma Valley," Dallas said. "A lot of Swiss and Italians came there and started growing grapes—"

Ellen got up quickly, some of the color going from her face. She was smiling gaily, too gaily, Hamp thought. "Of course I remember James Pitkin," she said as she passed Dallas's chair. "Didn't he marry that Lawford girl? What was her name?" She took the wine decanter from the table and set it on the oak sideboard at the far side of the room. For just a second Paul

180

Tremaine was looking at his sister and his mouth was ugly.

"What do you hear about the election, Dallas?" Hamp said. This was a safe subject and Ellen was grateful for it, but she was glad when Hamp and the Judge had finished and gone back outside. Paul found a chair in the big, bare living room and promptly went to sleep.

Dallas stayed and helped with the dishes and later he and Ellen had a second cup of coffee together. He acted as if the dinner had been a perfect success, but he was only being kind, Ellen knew. It bothered her that he should have to be kind to her. She had never before been in that position with an eligible male. She looked at Dallas quickly, the thought troubling her. A girl would have to be careful in this country. Homesickness and worry and a handsome man could be a bad combination. She knew that, but when Dallas suggested that perhaps he should be going she insisted he stay a little longer. She didn't want him to leave.

Out on the bunkhouse step Hamp smoked his fourth cigarette and watched the front door of the ranch house. "Is he gonna stay all night?" he said finally, throwing down his cigarette.

"Wouldn't know," Judge Norton said.

"Dusty would turn over in his grave," Hamp said.

"You ought to be glad," the Judge said, "Sue's rid of Dallas." The Judge was watching Hamp closely, and there was a little twinkle of devilment in his eyes.

"Women!" Hamp snorted.

"That's why I never married," the Judge said.

"Why?"

"Women."

Hamp rolled another cigarette and stood up, tall and lean, his jeans skin-tight, his feet small for the width of his shoulders. He wanted to talk to Ellen a moment. He wanted to reassure her about getting another haying crew. At least that's what he thought he wanted to talk to her about. The ranch-house door opened and Dallas and Ellen were silhouetted there for a moment. Hamp let the cigarette slip from his fingers.

Ellen and Dallas stood there together, saying good night, and then Ellen came out onto the porch, closing the door behind her, and now Hamp could see only their shapes, outlined by the light from the window. He knew Dallas was holding her hands and he could hear the faint murmur of voices, and then the two forms were moving closer together and Rombeck's head was bending down and Ellen's arms were reaching up. . . . Hamp's throat was constricted and tight.

"Well," Judge Norton said, "I reckon he's leaving now."

Dallas Rombeck came out toward the barn. He saw Hamp start for the house and he walked over to intercept him. "I wouldn't try to talk to her now, Hamp," he said. "She's upset."

The idea of Rombeck advising him angered Hamp, and then there was another anger, swifter, more deadly. He reached out and gripped Rombeck's arm. "You just have to talk so much, don't you, shyster?"

Rombeck jerked his arm free. "Don't you think she has a right to know?"

"If you knew Tuna was in town you must have known he was coming," Hamp accused. "So maybe she's got a right to know it was Boyd Novis who sent for him."

"All right," Dallas said. "She knows it. I've told you a dozen times I have no more regard for Boyd Novis personally than you have. In my business a man doesn't pick his clients because of their sterling character—"

"It must be a hell of a business," Hamp said. He walked swiftly toward the house.

Ellen heard him on the porch and opened the door before he had a chance to knock. For a moment she stood there, looking at him as if he were a stranger, a feeling that was almost revulsion touching her. Hamp pushed the door closed and stood there, his hat in his hands, the light throwing shadows across his face. If he would only say something, she thought. How could he be so calm, knowing a man is coming to kill him? "I suppose you'll want to be leaving," she said. "It's all right."

She saw the surprise in his eyes. "Leaving where, Miss Ellen?"

Paul Tremaine stirred in his chair and leaned forward, his hands gripped between his knees. "Tell you what, Dallas old man," Paul said. "Don't tell old moneybags Novis we won't sell. Leave the door open. Try to get him to raise the ante another thousand—"

Ellen ignored her brother. "You don't need to pretend," she said to Hamp. "Dallas told me all about Tuna Stinson. I'm glad he did." She couldn't bring herself to put it all into words—to say that Dallas had told her that the brother of the man Hamp had killed was back.

"Get him to raise it a thousand dollars, Dallas," Paul said. He sat up suddenly. "Oh, Hamp. Thought it was Dallas." He ran both hands through his hair and sat there, his head down.

"Don't just stand there," Ellen said, and now her voice was near the breaking point. She tried to picture in her mind what Tuna Stinson would be like—a man who had come with a gun to kill another man—and then she looked at Hamp, making herself realize that this man, too, had stalked and killed and perhaps would kill again or be killed. She couldn't control her horror and revulsion any longer. The tears came and the taste of them was in her throat. "Can't you say something?" she said. "What will you do?"

"I figgered I'd ride over and see those two squatter outfits just south of us tomorrow morning," he said. "I think I can get them to work in the hay for us."

She didn't want him to see her cry. She couldn't stand that. "Get out," she said. "Please go—" She turned swiftly so that her back was to him, and she opened the door and held it.

He went through the door, still holding his hat. Then he paused for a second and looked at her and she had to meet his eyes. Killer's eyes, she thought. . . . She closed the door and stood there, knowing she couldn't bear any more.

Paul's voice was thick with wine. "That's right," he said. "Turn on the tears. Little Brother got drunk."

A sob caught in her throat and she looked at her brother. His hair was mussed, his tie crooked, his face flushed. She thought of the hundred times she had gone through this, each time thinking she could never face it again, but now it was something tangible, something familiar. It was easier than trying to understand men who killed. "Paul, you promised," she said. "Everyone noticed it."

"And do you think I care what any of these yokels notice or think?" Paul lurched out of the chair and faced her belligerently. "How much longer are you going to stay in this hellhole? Do you know Boyd Novis has been after this place—God knows why—for a dozen years? Dallas will get us a good price for it."

Now she was angry and the anger was a

relief. "You'd like selling out, wouldn't you, Paul?" she said. "You'd like quitting before you even try, wouldn't you? You'd like it because then you'd never have to face the fact that you had failed."

His eyes cleared and they were hard with defensive anger. "That was a pleasant, sisterly thing to say."

"Perhaps it was, Paul," she said. "You made me say it."

He walked swiftly across the room toward her. "All right," he said, thrusting his face close. "Go ahead and say it. I'm a drunk. I'm, no good. I've never amounted to anything and I never will!"

"I didn't say that, Paul. But you did promise that this time you would try."

"Try what? Try to spit out of the middle of my mouth like Donnelly? I told you what I'd do with this place, didn't I? Sell it. Get some money out of it. Let's get back to civilization."

"And then what? The same people? The same drinking? The same gambling and losing it all and living off our friends? At least we don't have to take that humiliation here."

"Maybe you'd like to have me go out and shoot myself." These arguments always ended the same way. Always, in any argument, anything that called for decision, Paul would back down under a remark as childish as that one.

She bit her lip. "Go on to bed, Paul. We'll talk about it tomorrow."

She watched him go down the hall and heard him slam the bedroom door. When he was gone she sat down in a chair by the cold fireplace and started to cry. She cried for a long time, and when she looked up the chimney of the lamp was smoky and the room with its oak and leather furniture was gloomy and cold. Outside the night was alive with a thousand sounds. She looked at the elk horns in the dining room where the men hung their hats and she saw the loaded pistol there. She wanted to put it away, yet she was afraid to touch it. She looked at the black square of window and thought of two men with guns like that stalking each other like animals. . . .

In the bunkhouse Hamp Donnelly carefully cleaned a .45, a twin to the gun on the elk horns. He wiped off oil with a soft cloth and tried the gun twice in its plain leather holster. The light of the lantern was blood-

188

red against his face. "Getting late, Judge," Hamp said.

"She doesn't belong here, Hamp," the Judge said quietly. "She doesn't belong here any more than Paul does."

"I promised Dusty I'd try, didn't I?" Hamp Donnelly said. "You coming over tomorrow?"

"I'm not going home," the Judge said. "I'm staying here."

Hamp looked at his old friend. "It's between Tuna and me, Judge. You don't have to get mixed up in that part of it."

"I didn't say I did," the Judge said. There was a doublebarrel shotgun in the corner of the room. The Judge picked it up, broke it, and squinted down the twelve-gauge barrels. He went to a wooden box nailed on the wall and from the bottom shelf he took two shells and after weighing them once in his hand he shoved them into the gun and snapped the weapon closed. After that he set the gun by one of the bunks and kicked off his boots. He stretched his scrawny frame out on the bed, moving carefully, as if constantly aware of the brittleness of his bones. Lacing his hands behind his head, he stared up at the ceiling. "You know, Hamp," the Judge said, "I'm tired tonight."

Dallas Rombeck drove his rented red-wheel buggy toward Antelope with a growing impatience. He had wasted nearly three weeks and just tonight realized it for sure. When it came right down to signing the papers for the sale of Anchor, Paul wasn't going to have a thing to say about it. He was sure of that now. He cracked the lines against the buggy mare's back and it left dust tracks on the sleek hide.

Money. Damn, how it ground a man and pushed and squeezed. It seemed to him at this moment that there had never been a time in his life when he wasn't short of money. And just when a man got a little breathing space something always happened. Three times, previous to his coming to Antelope, he had made a start in the right direction, and always something had happened. There was that time in The Dalles when he and his law partner had really built up a clientele. They were beginning to get a lot of legal business from the River Transportation Company. But his partner had a young wife and the young wife felt she was neglected. He had been a fool, Dallas knew, but there was no use crying about it now. A scandal like that even in a town the size of The Dalles could ruin a man.

Perhaps he should have stayed in Portland. He was doing well there, but again it was a case of money. The people with whom he wanted to be identified—the people on the hill—never had to think about money, and the more he became involved with them, the deeper he went into debt. There were still a lot of unpaid bills in Portland. He thought of Jenette Apperson. Jenette with the blond hair and the soft eyes and the softer lips and a million dollars. He sighed deeply. He guessed he had been in love with Jenette. He had wanted to marry her. There was just the small matter of a million dollars and forty hard-headed Yankee relatives standing in the way of it. . . .

And now tonight he was going to have to face Boyd Novis again. "These things take time, Mr. Novis," he would say. "Perhaps if you increased the offer—say a thousand dollars—" It wouldn't work and Dallas knew it, and here was a fat commission slipping through his fingers, just as Sue Donnelly had said it would. He took out his handkerchief and wiped his lips. He was going to have trouble with Sue Donnelly too. He should never have gotten mixed up with her. She was too young, too emotional. She didn't understand that a man could have a future just by keeping on the good side of someone like Boyd Novis. And if he could manage the sale of Anchor he'd be in solid with Novis, Dallas knew. Why couldn't women be reasonable? He thought of Ellen Tremaine and he knew that now he was on the right track. If Boyd Novis wouldn't get too impatient.

As he drove down the poplar-lined street of the darkened town he saw the girl move away from the white picket fence and stand there. His first thought was that he would ignore her, but he couldn't do that. She would call out, call his name. He pulled the mare to a stop, and the girl ran out and stood by the off wheel, looking at him. "Sue, what on earth are you doing out here?"

"I had to talk to you. I've been waiting for two hours."

"Sue, this is silly."

"I had to know about Hamp. Is he all right? Is Tuna—"

Dallas felt a quick relief. "Hamp's all right. He can take care of himself, Sue. You mustn't worry about it."

"I saw Tuna leave town this evening. He took the shortcut trail over toward the river."

"Maybe he's going over to Condon. Maybe he's decided to forget it." It was totally dark here and she was just a form in the darkness and her voice was detached from reality, a worried voice reaching out for assurance. "You go to bed, Sue."

"Dallas, how much longer is this going on?"

"Sue, I can't tell. No one tells Hamp how to run his affairs. You know that."

"I don't mean that, Dallas. I mean us."

"Please, Sue. Let's don't start that. Not now."

"You're falling in love with her, aren't you?"

"Sue, be reasonable."

"But you are."

"It's just business, I tell you. Boyd Novis wants to buy Anchor, and if I can get Ellen to sell I'd be crazy not to. There's a good commission in it. I told you, Sue, I need money."

"Don't you ever get sick of kissing Boyd

Novis's feet? I know what you want, Dallas. You think Novis is going to run this country. You think you'll get a big job out of it."

"Sue, you're being impossible."

"Am I? I used to know you pretty well before she came here. You were in love with me once, remember?"

"Nothing's changed. As soon as I close this deal—"

"You're not going to close it, Dallas. I told you that right from the first. Anchor's not for sale, regardless of what you think. It's just going to wind up in another big fight." She stopped suddenly, as if she had already said too much.

"I have to go, Sue." Dallas clicked his tongue at the mare and the buggy rolled forward. He knew Sue was walking along beside the rig, her pace increasing with the speed of the buggy. He jerked the lines savagely. "Sue, please!"

"Let's go away like we planned, Dallas. Take me with you and we'll go someplace and start over."

"I can't do that."

"Because you're in love with her?"

"I've told you—"

"Get down and stand by me and tell me."

He sat there a moment, his teeth tightly

194

clenched, glad that she couldn't see his face. This could go on all night. He wrapped the lines around the whipstock and got down. She came into his arms, moving out of the darkness, clinging to him. "Dallas—Dallas—"

He brushed his lips close to her ear and turned her so he could look down the street toward the saloon. The light made a bright path across the street. He wondered if Boyd Novis would be at the saloon or at the hotel. "Don't worry so much, darling," he whispered. "Do you think I could ever forget you?" He tilted her head so that while he kissed her he could still watch the street. He felt her lips, eager and young, and he felt her fingers digging into his back. Dallas wondered if he should go to the saloon or to the hotel first. . . . The pressure of Sue's fingers relaxed and she pushed away from him. "There, darling," he said. "You see?"

She was standing close to him, her hands at her sides, her face tilted upward, a pale blot in the darkness. "Someday I'm going to learn to hate you, Dallas," she said quietly. "When I do it will be the happiest day of my life." She turned and walked into the darkness, and he heard the gate latch rise and fall.

He drove on down to the stable and turned in the rig, paying for it with the last money he had. The stableman blinked sleep from his eyes and pocketed the money. "Boyd Novis was lookin' for you," he said. "Said to tell you to come on up to the hotel."

"All right," Dallas said. He whipped dust from his coat and trousers with the back of his hand and recreased his beaver hat. He was a little tired of being at Novis's beck and call twenty-four hours a day, but a man had to sacrifice something for opportunity.

He crossed over to the hotel, and the night clerk, a thin-faced man with a green eyeshade looked up and saw him. "Mr. Novis wants to see you, Mr. Rombeck."

Dallas didn't answer. He crossed the sparsely furnished lobby and went up the stairs to the second floor. There was a light coming from under a door halfway down the hall. He went there and before he knocked he took a deep breath. The voice that asked him to come in was thin and dry.

It was a drab room, dingy and cluttered, and it went well with the small, almost dwarfed man who sat at a table playing solitaire. Boyd Novis glanced up, his eyes small and red-rimmed behind his thick-lens silver-rimmed glasses. His face was thin, his chin and jaws blue-black with a close-cropped beard. He had a large mouth and blue lips and his black hair was long and poorly groomed and there was dandruff on the shoulders of his black broadcloth coat. "Well?" he said.

There was a knock on the door, and Dallas was grateful for the interruption. He needed time to think. The door opened and the night clerk was there. The clerk kept opening and closing his hands with the uncertainty of a man afraid of his job. "Mr. Novis?"

"I'm listening."

"Mr. Novis, Joe over at the saloon says he run out of Meadowcreek rye and he wonders—"

Boyd Novis had risen to his feet. His lack of height was accented by the thick lifts he wore on his shoes. The lapels of his coat were stained and he wore a collar-band shirt without the collar. There were great smudged circles under his dark eyes. "I told you what to get, didn't I?"

The night clerk swallowed hard. "It wasn't my fault, Mr. Novis."

"Then find out whose fault it was," Boyd Novis said. "And get me a quart of

Meadow-creek rye, some water, and a glass."

"I'll sure try, Mr. Novis."

"You do that, Herman," Novis said. The clerk closed the door carefully and backed out into the hall. Boyd Novis shook his head. "Just a drink, that's all I wanted." He looked at Dallas and smiled. "Now what were you saying?"

"I think they're about ready to sell, Mr. Novis."

"You think?" Boyd Novis said.

"Well, it seems to me—"

"It seems?"

"Look, Mr. Novis, these things take time. I told you right from the first—"

"You got it wrong, Rombeck," Boyd Novis said. "You didn't tell me. I told you. I told you to buy Anchor. I told you how much to pay. I told you to buy it without raising a big fuss."

"Well, if you'll just be patient—"

"You tell that to my sheep, will you, Rombeck?" Novis said. "I'm overstocked and overgrazed now and I just bought two more bands from the Hawkins brothers down in Prineville. Those sheep will be here in a few days and I want graze for them when they get here."

"You should have held off awhile, Mr. Novis."

"You're telling me how to run my business?" Novis said. "I've made a half a million dollars, Rombeck. How much have you made?"

"If you'll just listen to me—"

"You listen to me, Rombeck," Novis said. He had placed his hands against the edge of the table. His fingers were bony and long, his nails dirty. He leaned forward, his eyes boring into Rombeck. "Do you know why I use you at all, Rombeck? Because it makes me feel good to talk about 'my attorney,' that's why. I like to see you strutting around in those fine clothes which my money bought. I like to think about you having that fine education and talking so pretty and all and then I think about how I didn't have nothing, how I started out as a sheepherder. That makes me feel good, Rombeck, but any time you don't jump when I say frog I can find something else to feel good about. Just remember, Rombeck, you need me but I don't need you. I was doing fine before you ever showed up." There was a timid knock on the door. "Come in, Herman," Novis said.

The night clerk sidled into the room. He

had a bottle and a pitcher of water and one glass. "I found some, Mr. Novis," he said eagerly. "Got it from that drummer in 27. It's got a couple of drinks gone, but it's Meadowcreek."

"You're a good boy, Herman," Novis said. Herman backed out, smiling gratefully. "There's a good boy, Rombeck," Novis said. "He gets what I send him after."

"If you'll let me explain—"

"There's nothing to explain, Rombeck," Novis said. He poured a meager amount of whiskey into a glass and filled the glass with water. He stood there, sloshing the thin, brown mixture. "I want Anchor. I get what I want." He took a small drink. "Like I told Tuna Stinson once, you should use kid gloves first. If that don't work, you can use a club." He took another drink. "By the way, did you know Tuna was going to herd sheep for me? I forgot if I told you."

"Mr. Novis, as your attorney, I think that was a mistake."

"And after your performance, what you think doesn't impress me," Novis said. He sipped his drink and his eyes were bright. "I hired Tuna to herd sheep, that's all. What he does outside of working hours is his business."

"But people will talk, Mr. Novis. You have to think about your position in this town. You can't afford to be connected with Tuna, Mr. Novis. You know what will happen between him and Hamp Donnelly—"

"And would it be so tragic if something happened to Donnelly?" Novis said. "Who does he think he is?" He peered through his glasses. "Matter of fact, Rombeck, maybe if Hamp Donnelly hadn't been around there you'd have had a lot more luck buying Anchor."

"Donnelly's tough, Mr. Novis. You've got no guarantee Tuna can whip him." Rombeck was sweating. He didn't like this. He didn't like it at all.

"I thought of that," Novis said. He tilted his glass and drained it slowly, and he set it down on the table. "I told Tuna to be careful." He smiled. "Money is a wonderful thing, Rombeck. You can even hire a man to be careful." He walked over and opened the door and held it, and as Dallas reached the hall and turned, completely frightened now, wanting to argue further, Novis smiled. "Oh, by the way, Rombeck. I nearly forgot."

"Yes, sir?"

"Unless you get some immediate action,

201

I don't see that there's any sense of me keeping you on a retainer, do you?"

Hamp Donnelly was fully awake. By the feel of the night and the quiet he knew it was nearly midnight. Like Judge Norton, he hadn't bothered to undress but had removed his boots and stretched out on the bunk, covering himself with a blanket. He lay there now, listening, knowing that some unusual sound had awakened him, unable to tell what it was.

He could hear the familiar noise of the horses moving around in the corral and he knew that that alone wouldn't have disturbed him. Someplace far oft a coyote yammered at a rising moon. Across the room Judge Norton's blankets moved and the old man's voice was a thin, phlegm-cracked whisper. "You awake, Hamp?"

"Yeah."

"Out by the barn," the Judge said.

"I'll take a look," Hamp said. He threw back the blankets, pulled on his boots, and his hand reached out and touched the familiar cedar butt of his gun. He thumbed back the hammer, and the click of it was loud in the silent room. With his forefinger he rolled the cylinder around to a loaded chamber and let the hammer down carefully. Then he thrust the weapon into the waistband of his trousers. The Judge moved from under his blankets, reaching for his shotgun.

Hamp opened the door carefully and stood there a minute, listening. A horse nickered a low complaint, as a horse does when reluctant to leave the home corral, and then there were hoofbeats, the sound of a horse walking, not in the dust of the corral but across the hard-packed yard. Hamp moved swiftly into the darkness, keeping close to the corral fence. He reached the side of the barn, edging his way along cautiously. He could see the rider, riding slowly out toward the main gate. He ran on around to the front of the barn. "Paul! Is that you, Paul?" The rider turned in his saddle, looking back, and then the horse gave a grunt of protest, as if he had been kicked hard or slapped with a quirt. There was a quick pound of hoofs and the horse was in a full gallop, heading up toward the short-cut trail that led to Antelope.

A light flared in the ranch house. The front door opened and Ellen's voice, high, charged with worry, called, "What is it?"

"It's nothing," Hamp said. "It's all right." He hurried back toward the bunkhouse, careless in his haste, and when he reached the edge of the corral he saw the quick blur of movement by the bunkhouse window.

Judge Norton's thin voice stung him like a whip. "Hamp! Watch it!"

There was a spurt of yellow flame, the crack of a sixshooter, and lead splintered the post a foot from Hamp's head. He heard Ellen Tremaine scream and he tugged the gun from his waistband, but now he was afraid to shoot, unable to see in the darkness, not knowing where Judge Norton was. The Judge's voice came again, floating across the space between the bunkhouse and the corral. "Drop it, Tuna, or I'll pull both these triggers at once!" There was a low curse, the sound of a heavy object hitting the ground. "I got him, Hamp," the Judge said.

Hamp started toward the bunkhouse and he heard Ellen running across the yard. "Get back in the house and stay there," he told her, his voice brusque.

He went on. The sky was thinning with the rising moon and now he could see Tuna Stinson standing there, his hands shoulder-high, a huge, hulking man, his features hidden in the darkness, a man who looked much like the brother Hamp Donnelly had killed. Hamp remembered those colorless eyes, the long, sandy hair that hung in rope-like strands from under the battered hat, the big mouth, slack and wide.

"He was by the window," Judge Norton said. "Figured he'd get you while you were asleep. He was playing it safe."

"Take that gun out of my back, old man," Tuna Stinson said. His voice was low in his throat. "Take that gun out of my back and I'll kill him. I'll kill him with my hands."

"You're through killing anybody, Tuna," the Judge said.

"I'll kill him—" It was only a rush of movement in the darkness, a swift sweep of sound as Tuna's hands came down and that tremendous shape was hurtling forward. Hamp felt the crushing impact, felt the breath go from his lungs. His fist lashed out and landed solidly. There was a grunt of pain and Tuna was rushing in, clubbing down with both fists, and Ellen was there, screaming at them to stop. The horses in the corral, bunched from the shock of the gunshot, snorted and shied and crowded against the fence. Tuna's shoulder caught Hamp in the chest and they were down, their arms locked, rolling in the dust.

The world exploded in a red mist when Tuna's fist landed against Hamp's temple. Hamp groped with his hands, trying to find Tuna's throat, and again that fist smashed down. There was blood in Hamp's mouth. He felt as if every tooth in his head had been jarred loose.

Hamp kicked with his feet and felt savage joy at Tuna's curse of pain. Hamp was on top now, slugging with his fists. He had taken the best Tuna had to offer, he knew that now, and the knowledge of it gave him a second wind, a second strength.

Tuna was twisting and turning, his thumb gouging for Hamp's eye. His thumb slipped, the nail ripping across Hamp's cheek, the thumb catching the corner of Hamp's mouth. There was no sound except their breathing, a strangled, choking, coughing sound.

They lay there that way, straining against each other, until Hamp got his right hand free, and he drove it down into the hollow of Tuna's throat. He hit again and again, the jar of his blows tearing with a white-hot pain through the bones of his arm until finally he knew there was no resistance. Tuna was lying there, his head rolling from side to side with the blows.

Hamp pushed himself free and stood up, his legs trembling with fatigue. Blood was running down his face and dripping on his chest. He had lost his gun. He stood there, breathing through his mouth, sucking in great gulps of air, completely oblivious of his surroundings. The light was gray and eerie and the dust cloud settled around his feet. Judge Norton, his face as thin as the blade of a hatchet, stood there holding a double-barrel shotgun. And Ellen was there, a dressing gown drawn tightly around her. Hamp could see her face. He lowered his eyes, not wanting to see what he had seen there before, and he saw Tuna Stinson lying there on the ground.

He heard Tuna moan and saw him roll over. Almost too late, he saw Tuna's left hand reach out. There was a glint of metal. Hamp's boot rose and crushed down against Tuna's left hand. He felt the flesh tear, felt the fingers open. He tromped down again and now he reached down and gripped Tuna by the shirt collar and jerked him to his feet.

Hamp realized then that Ellen was pushing between them, saying only one word, "Don't—" Her arms were holding Hamp's arms to his side, and Tuna Stinson was staggering away.

Hamp watched Tuna stumble into the night, disappearing into the darkness of the wind-break poplars around the house. In a moment a horse and rider came out. Tuna was leaning across the saddle horn, hunched over like a sick man, his head bobbing crazily on his short, thick neck. "Don't let him go, Hamp," Judge Norton said softly. "You're crazy if you let him go."

The girl held Hamp's arms tightly. "Please."

Hamp shook his head and his brain cleared. Ellen was standing close to him, her arms holding his arms against his side. She was looking up at him and he could see her face, but he couldn't see her eyes. He remembered how she had looked at him last night. "All right," he said. He pushed away from her and went to the back of the house where the water bucket and basin stood on the bench. He poured the basin full and doused his head, and his face and the water turned red with his own blood.

He could hear Ellen moving around inside the house and he heard her calling Paul's name, softly at first, then frantically. The back door opened and she stood there. "Paul's gone!"

"I know, Miss Ellen," Hamp said quietly. "I was fixin' to go after him."

She looked at him and saw his battered mouth and the wicked gash that ran from his temple to his chin. Judge Norton was there too, appearing out of nowhere as he often did. She stared at these two men and she could still hear Hamp's quiet voice saying, "I know, Miss Ellen. I was fixin' to go after him." What did Hamp know? She knew then that he knew everything there was to know about Paul. He had known from the first, known every weakness that Ellen knew, but he wasn't criticizing, any more than she had criticized. He knew Paul, and he was trying to help. . . .

She looked at Hamp Donnelly, remembering that this man had killed, remembering the brutality of the fight, remembering the revulsion and horror she had felt. She still felt it, but it was detached feeling, and her concern for Paul was real. Again Hamp

Donnelly was two men. One she hated—the one who had killed. The other she needed—this quiet one who was always present, always ready to help. She thought of Paul and knew she couldn't wait this out alone. Not this time, because this time had to be the last time. She had promised herself that. Always before some mutual friend stayed to bring Paul home and make excuses; someone they had known for years bailed Paul out of jail and failed to mention it again. But this was different. This was a new place. These men were strangers, and Paul would have to stand up as a man on his own. She shook her head. "No, Hamp. Don't go after him. Not this time. He's a grown man and it's time he works things out for himself."

She saw Hamp's face, battered and torn, and she tried to think of it as a killer's face, but for this moment it wasn't that. "I think that's best, Miss Ellen," Hamp said. "A man needs to make up his own mind about things."

The gray light of morning was everywhere, a harsh, cold light with no softness about it. She looked at Hamp and the Judge and forced herself to realize that these men were her friends. "Here," she said, "let me help you." She dampened a towel and wiped the blood from the cuts on Hamp's face. And once, when her face was close to his, she saw his eyes and for a second she was held by what she saw there. She lowered her gaze and worked swiftly. "I'll bandage your hand," she said. "It's badly hurt."

―――――――――――――――――――――――――17

Paul Tremaine had awakened with a brutal headache and the dry, cottony taste of a wine hangover in his mouth. He raised up on his elbows and the bed moved sickeningly. After a while he got his feet on the floor and he sat there on the edge of the bed, holding his face in his hands, and the hot, burning thirst in his mouth spread and now it was in his stomach and he had to have something to drink.

He thought of the bucket of cold water in the kitchen and he started toward the door, unsteady on his feet. He didn't want to awaken Ellen. He didn't want to talk to her. He had talked to her too many times. The room was hot and stuffy, even though the night was cool. He'd go back to bed, he decided, and last it out until morning.

The thirst grew and tore at him and he

knew he had to have whiskey to put out the fire. Just one drink, he thought, that was all, and then he could sleep. A feeling of helpless terror started growing inside him. There wasn't any whiskey in the house. Ellen had seen to that. She didn't trust him.

The more he thought about it, the more his panic grew, and now he knew there was no sense trying to sleep. He got one leg into his trousers and stumbled trying to get the other one in. He put on his shoes and buttoned his collar. It choked him, so he unbuttoned it again. No, he decided. Not this time. This time he wouldn't take that first drink.

His stomach kept crying out for it and his brain kept telling him he didn't want it. He'd battle it out. For a half hour then he paced up and down the room, his tongue thick, his mouth horribly dry. He was cold and he dressed, putting on his coat. He had to have a drink of water. He opened the door into the hall carefully and walked slowly on tiptoe up the hall to the living room and turned left into the dining room. He stumbled against a chair and stood there, his heart pounding, waiting for Ellen to call out. There was no sound and there was nothing outside but the maddening chirp of a cricket, which only accented the silence he hated.

He went to the kitchen and drank greedily, direct from the bucket, spilling water down his chest. After a moment he felt a pleasant giddiness. Maybe a breath of fresh air would help. Moving stealthily, he let himself out the back door.

He walked toward the barn, the cool, night air pleasant against his skin. It was completely dark, a darkness that funneled in on him and made him a focal point. He stood by the barn door a long time, and the longer he stood there, the more he felt alone. If there were only someone to talk to. It was the silence of this place . . .

He thought of the little town of Antelope and tried to remember just how far away it was and he thought of it in measures of time and not of miles. He wondered what time it was. Eleven, maybe. He wanted a cigarette but be didn't have any. He smoked tailor-made Sweet Caporals and Ellen had brought him some from town. He'd go into the house and get some. . . . He took two steps and knew that he couldn't go back there and be alone in that house. He tried to spit and there was no saliva in his mouth.

In the corral a horse nickered softly. Paul Tremaine made up his mind. He ran to the corral and opened the gate and went inside. His heart was pounding fiercely and he was nearly sobbing. He tried to catch one of the horses, but they shied away from him. He went to the barn and found a thick hair rope, and he ran back and managed to get one of the horses in a corner. He slipped the rope around the animal's neck.

There were four saddles in the barn. He took the first one. He worked furiously, his thirst growing with his exertion, and he pulled himself into the saddle. He was hatless, and the cold of the night chilled through his suit coat. He didn't want to awaken Ellen. He couldn't do that. He started riding slowly, holding in on the horse's reins. He was halfway to the gate when he heard Hamp Donnelly calling his name. Paul glanced back. He dug his heels in and slapped the horse on the shoulder with the long ends of the reins. The animal lurched forward and Paul gripped the saddle horn, and then the horse was in a long, smooth gallop, heading for the short-cut trail to Antelope. Behind him there was a shot and Paul felt a sudden terror. He kicked the horse with all his strength.

He had no sense of time or distance. He saw the dark shape of the butte, the butte with the flat top where his uncle was buried. He felt as if someone were behind him, staring at him. Below, in the little valley, a pair of yellow lights flickered off and on through the swaying poplars. He rode on down the hill, the horse stumbling now. Someone was still up in Antelope. Someone who would talk to him.

He came into town on a full run, the horse streaked with foam, its breathing loud in the night. A dozen dogs started barking and someplace a baby cried and a light flared on in the window. At the far end of the street the windows of the hotel laid a yellow pattern on the dust, and across from that two horses were tied at a hitch rail. He rode there and he saw the faded sign of the Elkhorn Saloon.

He dismounted carefully and forced himself to walk across the board porch. He wanted to go back now. He really did. But he couldn't. The horse had to rest. He walked into the saloon. He had expected to see Clete behind the bar. It was another man. The bartender gave Paul a brief, uninterested glance. Two men playing cards at a table looked up. They were two of the men who had cut hay on Anchor and quit to go to work for Boyd Novis. There was no one else in the place. To hell with you, Paul thought. To hell with all three of you. He moved over to the bar and laid down a silver dollar—the only money he had. "Clete here?" Paul said.

"Clete owns the place," the bartender said. "He don't have to work nights."

"Can a man buy a drink here?" Paul said.

The bartender said nothing. He was a fat man with a round face and eyes that had seen too many drunks. They always came in about this time, the ones with the black horrors. The ones who couldn't sleep without a drink, and one drink would lead to ten and then they would be off again. He knew this was Paul Tremaine, but that didn't surprise him. Nothing surprised the bartender any more. He got a bottle and shot glass and shoved them out on the bar, tiredly. Three drinks, usually, then they started to talk. They started to tell all about themselves. The bartender yawned. After that they wanted to borrow money. Just until tomorrow. Changed my pants and forgot to take my money. The bartender stretched and yawned again. It would be all right, he supposed. He'd give this one twenty or so on an IOU. He didn't know much about Paul; he didn't know much about Ellen. But that was all right. Hamp would make it good. . . . The bartender watched Paul take his third drink. Here it comes, he thought.

At the table Boyd Novis's two sheepherders shuffled the cards. They had been waiting for Tuna Stinson. He was supposed to come in and have a game with them. The bartender glanced at the Seth Thomas clock on the wall. Pretty late. Three more hours and he'd close this fire trap and get some sleep. Paul Tremaine was talking now and the bartender was answering, but he wasn't hearing anything. They all said the same thing; they all wanted the same answers. "Sure," he said finally. "I knew your uncle well. Fine man." He tossed a pad and a pencil on the bar. "Just give me an IOU. Like I said, I don't own the place. I got to have something to put in the till."

A half hour later Paul Tremaine was playing poker with Boyd Novis's two sheepherders. The butterflies were gone from his stomach. His brain was keen and sharp. It was good to have someone to talk to. Even sheepherders. He had another drink and laughed at a poor joke. After all, what was supposed to be wrong with sheepherders? The cards made a whispering sound against the green top of the table. In back of the bar the bartender reached down inside his shirt, scratched his back, and yawned. It was a hell of a life, he decided.

The sunlight was red in the kitchen windows. Ellen had dressed and brushed her hair. She put more wood in the stove and started a second pot of coffee. The thin fragrance of cigarette smoke came from the dining room, where Hamp and Judge Norton were finishing their breakfast.

She was waiting again, just as she had waited so many times, but this time it was different. This time she was not waiting alone. For years now she had tried to cover up for Paul, feeling she could never stand the humiliation of anyone knowing. But Hamp knew and Judge Norton knew and they had known all along—perhaps even before Ellen and Paul had come here. There was no sense of humiliation about it at all. Rather it was a sense of security, a sense of having someone to share her worry and help her with it.

She glanced through the door and saw Hamp sitting there, his chair directly beneath the elk horns, and she saw her uncle's gun in its holster. Yesterday when she had looked at that gun she had thought of Hamp and of how he had killed a man and she had wondered if she could face him again, knowing that about him. Now even that feeling was gone. It didn't seem to matter in the same way. As Hamp had said, a man had to make up his own mind about things.

Last night seemed like an age ago, a different world. The fact that Paul had gotten drunk did not set the night aside and give it shape. It was just one more night in a hundred nights. She thought of Dallas Rombeck and her pulse quickened. In a way she felt cheap about letting him kiss her. It had been one of those things—she at an emotional breaking point, he sympathetic, understanding. She had no real feeling for Dallas except that he had tried to be a friend to Paul, she told herself. It was only appreciation. But there was a small excitement in her. Making excuses like that was the first danger signal, and she knew it.

Through the window she could see the rolling hills and the winding silver of the river. Yesterday she had hated it; today she didn't. There was no way to explain it. Unless it could be that she had found two things she had never known, two things she had needed. She could have Dallas Rombeck's love, she felt sure of that. And with Hamp and the Judge to help her she had a security that had been lacking all her life. She could even forgive Hamp for his fight. A man had a right to fight for his life.

She could understand that now. She couldn't understand how a man could kill, but she could understand how a man could fight. In a way she was making Paul fight for his life. It couldn't be accomplished all at once. He was in town now, undoubtedly. He was probably getting drunk. But she had decided to let him fight this one out himself and when he came home, repentant, contrite as he always was, she would say as little as possible. But she wouldn't back down. Not this time. She would stay here and Paul would make a go of Anchor and she would help him. When he had succeeded, then would be time enough to think of Dallas Rombeck. She opened a window and the fragrance of the land came into the room.

Hamp brought the dishes in from the dining room and set them on the sink. The red sun against his face accented the bruises and abrasions. The bandage on his left hand was working loose and she took his hand

and retied it, saying nothing until she was finished. He turned his hand and looked at the bandage. "You said last night you thought you could get those farmers south of us to work in the hay," she said.

"I think so," he said.

"All right," she said. "See what you can do. We have to get the hay in."

She met his eyes and she realized that without telling him anything she had told him what she had decided. She tried to read what she saw in his eyes and decided it was pride. It made her feel humble and strong at the same time. She wished she could tell him that Dallas Rombeck had had a part in this decision. Hamp's lips were battered and swollen, but he was smiling. "All right, boss," he said. He took his hat from the elk horns and crossed the yard toward the barn, walking with a long, determined stride.

Judge Norton's voice didn't seem so cracked and dry as usual. It was fuller, rounder. "Your uncle would have been proud of you, Ellen." She didn't answer. She walked across the living room and stared out the west window, and from here she could see the road lifting up to the summit and she could see the butte with the flat the flat top. She thought of the grave that was there and she thought of the town beyond and of Paul. She came back to the dining-room table and sat down and waited.

———————————————————————18

Ellen was grateful for the company of Judge Norton. The old man talked with an old man's balance, the present playing against the past, Antelope and Anchor and the surrounding country becoming a world. He told her things about her uncle that she had never known until finally she could understand Dusty, a man with dreams and ideals. The Judge was drawing a picture of Hamp, too, and she wanted to know more. "Tell me about Orvie Stinson," she said. She was no longer afraid to hear it.

He told her the story carefully, making her see every detail of it. "Hamp always felt Orvie was responsible for your uncle's death," the Judge said. "But even before that it was Orvie or Hamp, one. Orvie was mean. He would have shot Hamp in the back one day, sure. It didn't take the judge long to see that. They turned Hamp loose and I guess it was Boyd Novis talked Tuna into leaving town for a while."

"So it isn't over for Hamp, is it?" she said. "He's right back where he started. Whipping a man like Tuna Stinson with fists isn't enough."

"That's right," the Judge said. "It isn't enough."

"I'll be glad when we get the hay in," she said. She went out to the kitchen and stirred up the fire and made more coffee, and for a long time she stood there looking out the window, looking at Anchor. Here it has to be the big fight, she thought. Here it has to be all the way. . . .

"There are some other things I want to tell you," the Judge said. An hour had gone and she was sitting across from him, sitting so that she could look out the window and see the road that led up the hill and by the butte. "Even after I retired I took care of your uncle's legal work, you know."

"I know." She put her finger against the handle of the cup and turned the cup around in its saucer. "My uncle thought a lot of Hamp, didn't he?"

"He loved him like a son," the Judge said.

"I've always wondered why he didn't leave Anchor to Hamp."

"I guess he did," the Judge said. He was watching her closely. "Depends on how you look at it. He told you to keep him on as foreman, didn't he?"

"A hundred times."

"A man like Hamp doesn't need to own land or cattle," the Judge said. "He's here and things are going the way Dusty wanted them to go. For Hamp that's enough."

"Yes," she said quietly. "I suppose it is." She was surprised that the thought distressed her. Hamp Donnelly would never need anything more than this. Nor would he ever need anyone.

"He's proved that," the Judge said. "He could have had Anchor if he had wanted it. He could have discouraged you, made you want to give it up."

She only half heard at first, and then suddenly the words reached her. She looked at the Judge, realizing he was trying to tell her something he had wanted to tell her for a long time. "I don't understand."

"Didn't you ever think it was odd a man like your uncle didn't leave a formal will?"

"I had all his letters," she said. "I spent that month here with him, talking about it. He always said he wanted Paul and me to have the place. There was no one to contest it."

"He did leave a will, Ellen. I have it."

She couldn't decide what he was trying to tell her. "But if that's so—"

"Hamp wouldn't let me probate it." The Judge reached out and touched her hand. "You see, Ellen, Dusty wanted the ranch to belong to you and Paul, all right. He wanted that because you are Tremaines. But there was always the chance you wouldn't like it or that Paul wouldn't straighten out." He shrugged. "Dusty didn't want Anchor sold, Ellen. It meant too much to him. That was the really important thing. He made sure in his will it would always belong to someone who wanted it the way he wanted it."

She stood up, the color draining from her face. "What are you trying to tell me?"

"Hamp wouldn't let me probate the will because be thought it wouldn't be fair to Paul. He was afraid it would make Paul feel he was on trial." The Judge stood beside her, a thin little man, trying to be kind. "Dusty knew all about Paul, Ellen. He knew it the first time he came back to Philadelphia to see you; I can see that now. He left it up to Hamp to work it out, and if it didn't work out he wanted Anchor to go to Hamp."

"He wouldn't do that," Ellen said. "He

couldn't trust a man that much. Not any man."

"He could trust Hamp Donnelly that much, Ellen."

Ellen sat down. Now so many things made sense. The dogged persistence of Hamp; the way he had tried to make her see beauty in this land. His thinly masked dislike for Dallas. "Yes," she said, "I suppose he could."

She looked through the window toward the road. A buggy topped the summit and started down the hill, the dust of its wheels rising and forming a thin curtain of pink transparency across the front of the butte where Dusty Tremaine was buried. She knew it was Dallas Rombeck and she knew he would be bringing Paul home.

She felt the dead weight of disappointment. It was like being back in Philadelphia, trying to hide Paul's escapades from people, having friends be kind and considerate, pretending to be blind, wounding with their very consideration.

"I wouldn't have told you, Ellen," the Judge said, "but this morning I knew it would be all right. I knew you would stay regardless of what happened."

Yes, she thought, regardless of what happened. She went outside and waited there in the yard. Don't be kind, Dallas, she thought. If you really care for me, don't be kind. She wished that anyone but Dallas could have been the one to see Paul like this, and then she didn't care. If Dallas loved her it wouldn't make any difference.

Dallas didn't offer sympathy, and she was glad for that. Paul was slumped in the seat, his face bloated, his mouth open, his suit coat stained with his own sickness. She stood aside while Dallas and the Judge got him out of the buggy and led him into the house. "A full house," Paul mumbled as they sat him in the living room. "How could he beat a full house?"

"Ellen, I don't like to tell you this—" Dallas was cracking the knuckles of his hands.

"Gambling?"

"That's right."

"How much?"

"Two thousand, Ellen."

"To you?"

"Of course not, Ellen," Dallas said, and she was sorry she had said that. "A couple of sheepherders."

"Pretty big game for sheepherders, isn't it?" Judge Norton said.

"I suppose it was," Dallas said, "but it

227

won't keep them from collecting. If they had lost they would have paid off. I made sure of that."

"You mean Boyd Novis would have paid off for them?" the Judge said.

"Novis backs his men up, Judge. You know that."

"Where it will do him some good," the Judge said.

"Ellen, I hate this." Dallas took a handkerchief from his pocket and mopped his face.

"It's not your fault," Ellen said. "Anyway, we'll pay, somehow. Maybe Paul will have to herd sheep, but we'll pay."

"You don't have to pay, Ellen," the Judge said quietly. "The man was drunk. He didn't know what he was doing."

"He signed an IOU," Dallas said.

"Suppose he did? You can't collect it." There was anger in the Judge's voice.

"Judge, don't be a fool," Dallas said bluntly. "They'll take it out of Paul's skin and you know it. Those sheepherders were friends of Tuna Stinson's."

Ellen thought of that hulking shape she had seen in the darkness and she thought of him riding away into the night like a wounded animal. "I said we'd pay," she said.

"Ellen, why don't you get out of this?" Dallas said. "This is no place for you or Paul either." He came close to her and put his arm around her. "Go ahead and sell out and let Boyd Novis worry about whether or not he'll pay this IOU. I talked to him this morning and he's willing to settle with the two men."

"If Ellen sells Anchor to him, is that it?" the Judge said.

"I'm only trying to do what's best for Ellen and Paul," Dallas snapped.

"And make a fat commission for yourself," the Judge said.

The color flooded into Rombeck's face, but he didn't lose his poise. "I could take care of the sale of Anchor for you, Ellen. You could take a stage out of this place tomorrow."

"I'm afraid not, Dallas," she said.

"But don't you realize what you're doing to Paul? Those men won't wait for their money. This isn't Philadelphia, Ellen. Men have been killed over gambling debts." Dallas had hoped he wouldn't have to go this far. He had hated the assignment right from the first—hated it when Boyd Novis had called him to his room and shown him the IOU—hated the smugness and certainty he had seen in Boyd Novis's pinched face. He had felt like a fool, hauling Paul out of the saloon where he had slept all night, signing a release for Ned Crockett, the marshal. And he had hated most having Sue Donnelly see him, for he hadn't fooled Sue. She had known he was crawling for Boyd Novis again. "You've got to for Paul's sake, Ellen."

"I can't, Dallas," Ellen said. "Anchor isn't mine to sell."

"Well, Paul, then—"

"It isn't Paul's either," Ellen said. "It belongs to Hamp Donnelly."

It took a moment for that to sink in, and even then it meant nothing to Dallas. He looked at Ellen and then at the Judge, and he saw satisfaction in the Judge's eyes. Dallas beat down a rising panic. This was his last chance and he knew it. Boyd Novis had made that plain. He thought of the weeks he had spent licking Boyd Novis's boots, confident that it would pay off—sure that Boyd Novis would grow and continue to grow and a man who kept close to him would grow with him. "I don't know what you're talking about." He had trouble with his voice.

"About Anchor, Dallas," the Judge said.

"It's not for sale to anyone except Hamp. I've got Dusty's will to back it up."

"There wasn't any will," Dallas said, his voice rising. He looked at Paul slumped in the chair, and he thought of how he had hauled Paul out of the saloon with everyone watching, humbling himself. He remembered the way Boyd Novis had shoved him around. "I saw what papers there were, Ellen. I helped you with them."

"There was a will, Dallas," she said.

"Then it's no good," he said. He knew he was shouting, but he couldn't stop it. "It hasn't been probated. It won't hold.'"

"If it held with Hamp Donnelly, Dallas," Ellen said, "it would hold with me."

Dallas's panic was complete. Everything he had worked for was going to smash. And there was Sue . . . He would have to face Sue. . . .

The Judge said, "Tell Novis it didn't work, Dallas."

"But Paul," Dallas said. "Ellen, can't you see Paul's in danger?"

"Paul will have to decide about that, Dallas," Ellen said.

Dallas felt the perspiration running down his back. They couldn't do this to him. It meant too much. It meant everything. Only last night he had been so close. He had kissed Ellen and held her in his arms. He knew she trusted him. . . . He forced himself to calm down and smile. "All right, Ellen," he said. "I only want to help you and I thought this was the best way. If you want to stay and fight it out, I want you to know I'll be with you. Whatever you do, I want to help you."

"I appreciate that, Dallas," she said. "More than you know."

"It hasn't been easy for me, trying to keep this on a business basis, knowing if I did sell Anchor for you you'd be leaving here." Dallas had complete control of himself now. "It was the only way I knew to do what I thought was best for you and Paul, but the idea of you leaving has driven me crazy—" He took both her hands in his and stood there looking down at her.

"You've been kind, Dallas." He saw the curve of her lips and the pulse in her throat. The pressure of his fingers tightened around her hands and he felt a surge of confidence.

"Surely you know why, Ellen," he said softly. "After last night you must know why." He pulled her toward him and saw the surprise in her eyes. He knew he would have to be careful. . . .

Ellen felt the pulse in her throat, and the intensity of his voice touched her. She was tired of being alone. So tired of it . . . She would have let him take her in his arms, but the Judge was standing there, listening to this, and she saw Paul, slumped in his chair, watching with bloodshot eyes as Dallas put his arm around her. It was suddenly cheap and tawdry. She twisted aside. "Don't, Dallas—"

"I have to, Ellen," he said. "I can't keep quiet any longer. I want to marry you, Ellen."

She hesitated, knowing she had wanted to hear those words, but everything was wrong. "Please, Dallas—"

"We can work this out together, Ellen. For Paul's sake. I know these people. I know Boyd Novis. Please, Ellen. I love you. I can work everything out—"

"I suppose you could," Judge Norton said disgustedly. "You could sell off the cattle and lease the land to Boyd Novis, maybe."

Dallas whirled, his mouth hard. "Get out, will you? Haven't you any decency at all?"

"You'd double-cross your own mother,

233

wouldn't you, Rombeck? You've kissed Novis's feet, hoping he'd get you a political job, and now that you can't produce for him you figure you'll marry Anchor and hold Novis up for it—"

"Judge, I'll handle this," Ellen said, frightened. The men's voices were almost shouts.

"Get out of here." Dallas was suddenly deadly calm. He started moving toward the Judge, his fists clenched at his sides.

"Have you told Sue Donnelly about your plans?" the Judge taunted. "Or did you just dream this one up when you found out Anchor wasn't for sale?"

"Shut your lying mouth!" Dallas Rombeck's arm drew back and lashed out, sending the old man crashing back against the wall. The Judge raised a thin, shaking hand and touched the blood that had started from his nose.

"You dirty, rotten rat," the Judge said softly. "The only decent thing you ever did in your life was to throw Sue over."

Dallas lunged forward. He had the Judge by the throat and was holding him up as his fist drove in. Paul stumbled to his feet, his eyes furious.

Ellen didn't cry out. The disgust she felt

was too great for that. She saw Dallas turn and throw the Judge halfway across the room and she saw the old man crumble there. "Ellen, listen to me—" Dallas was coming toward her.

She started to back away. She saw Paul try to stop Dallas, saw Dallas push him aside, and Paul fell back into the chair. She backed across the dining room, pushing a chair in front of her, and then she was against the wall, directly under the elk horns. "Ellen, you don't understand!"

"I understand everything now," she said. Her hand reached up and back, and the holstered .45 that belonged to her uncle was there. She gripped it and pulled it free of the holster. It was heavy. She held it with both hands and pulled back the hammer. "Get out, Dallas."

"Ellen, don't be a fool!"

"Get out," she said. "Get out before I kill you!"

It was all a blind haze. She knew Dallas had gone, and she heard the buggy, the wheels grating and rattling as the horse broke into a run. Now she knew how it was that a man could kill. . . . The violence of her emotion left her weak and trembling. Dust came in through the open door, and she was on her knees by the Judge, the gun forgotten on the table. The Judge was unconscious, a cut on his head where it had hit the floor. She looked up and Paul was standing there. He seemed sober and older and his eyes were clear. He reached down and pulled her to her feet.

He stood there a second, looking deep into her eyes, and then he kissed her. "I'll take care of this, Ellen," he said. He started toward the door.

"Paul, don't leave me!"

"You said once I never finished anything I started, Ellen. You were right. It's about time I finish something, Ellen. I'm going to straighten this out with Novis myself."

There was something in Paul's voice that frightened her and at the same time reassured her—a new strength, almost as if Paul had finally grown up, a man who could make a decision. The Judge moaned and she turned toward him, and when she looked again Paul was gone. She ran to the door and called to him, but he didn't answer. She knew he was in the barn, saddling a horse. She ran back to the Judge, afraid to leave him now, afraid he might die. She got a basin and towel and bathed the Judge's face. She lifted his head, and it was like lifting the head of a child. . . . She saw Paul ride through the gate and take the short-cut trail toward town. It wasn't until he was gone that she realized her uncle's gun was missing.

---**19**

Hamp Donnelly hired two men and two sixteen-year-old boys to work in the hay. It wasn't much of a crew, but it would do all right. There was a singing inside Hamp that wouldn't go away even when he thought of Tuna Stinson and the gun fight that would have to come. Nothing had changed so far as his fight with Tuna was concerned, but something else had changed. The most important thing of all. Even when it did happen with Tuna he felt now he could face Ellen and explain. Perhaps then he wouldn't see the one thing he feared in her eyes. Last night, he knew, had made a difference.

He was in love with Ellen. He knew that and he no longer tried to deny it. He wondered how he would tell her of his love or if he ever would. He knew that from now on just being on Anchor, working things out the way Dusty had wanted them, wouldn't be enough. He rode into Anchor headquarters about three in the afternoon.

He sensed something wrong even before he dismounted. Then he saw Ellen running toward him, calling his name. He threw himself out of the saddle and started toward her, and she came into his arms, sobbing against his chest, saying his name over and over. He let his hand caress her hair and he held her close, wanting never to let her go. "It's all right," he said softly. "Whatever it is, it's all right."

He led her toward the house, his arm around her, and bit by bit she told him, told him everything. He felt his anger mounting. He went into the house and the Judge was there, stretched out on the divan, a cold cloth pressed against his face. "Take care of him, Ellen," Hamp said. She turned toward him, and there was no pretense between them. He kissed her swiftly and hurried outside. He knew she was following him.

"I'm going with you," she said behind him.

"You better not, Ellen."

"It's our fight," she said. "Yours and mine. I'm going with you." She met his eyes, and he saw she was no longer afraid of him and he knew she never would be again.

He fought to control his excitement. She understood now. Understood how it was that a man might have to kill. He would never have to explain. Last night she had looked at him as if he were an outcast; now, for the first time, she was accepting him as he was. She wanted to go with him and she had a right to go. . . . "I'll hitch up the buckboard, then," he said.

He coaxed all the speed there was out of the team, running them where the road dipped on a downgrade, walking them on the steeper pulls. At the summit he stopped to let them rest. He hadn't spoken a word since leaving the ranch. Ellen sat beside him, her right hand gripping the iron hand rail, her left hand clenched against the edge of the seat board. Over his shoulder Hamp saw the butte, dancing with afternoon sun now, the shadow a pool of blue directly under its own bluffs. The horses stood with muscles quivering, sweat dripping from their bellies. He walked them slowly for half a mile and then whipped them into a run down the slope toward Antelope.

They passed the schoolhouse and he

slowed the team. He knew there was trouble here. It was in the vacant schoolyard and it lay on the dust of the street and lurked in the death-still leaves of the poplars. There was a crowd in the street down near Paxton's store. Hamp pulled the team into the shade and wrapped the lines around the brake. "You wait here," he said, and she remembered another time he had told her to wait. He climbed down and walked down the center of the street. The holstered gun slapped against his thigh.

A woman was standing to one side, crying, and Sue was there, trying to keep the children back. He met Sue's eyes and saw the warning, and then he was pushing his way through the crowd, elbowing them aside. He heard a soft curse. Ned Crockett, the marshal, stood inside the circle, trying to push people back. A kid kept jumping up and down, trying to see over the head of the man in front of him. A body lay in the street, and the blood was black on the dust. It was Paul, and he was dead.

Hamp felt the sickness turn in his stomach and then the crowd was pushing, surging against him, and Ellen was there. He tried to stop her. He tried to hold her and hide her face against his chest. She pulled away from him and she was down in the dust. He heard her voice, broken and crying, crying out as if to an injured child. "Paul— Paul—" Hamp's anger rose to white heat, and when he moved back through the crowd they parted and made an aisle and let him through. He saw Jake Paxton and a dozen men he knew, and their faces were blurs.

"Tremaine come ridin' into town like a madman." It was Jake Paxton talking to him, talking with a hushed voice, his words rushing. "He wanted to see Boyd Novis. God, Hamp, it was like Dusty himself, the way Paul walked up the street. He met Novis right there where he's layin'. Tuna was with Novis. Tremaine said something and reached into his pocket and Tuna drew on him. Tremaine had a gun all right, but God, Hamp, Paul didn't have a chance against Tuna—"

The marshal came out of the crowd. He put his hand on Hamp's arm. "Take it easy, Hamp."

"Where's Tuna?" Hamp said.

"He's in the hotel. I've got it covered, Hamp. He can't get out. Hamp! Wait a minute!" The marshal gripped Hamp's arm and spun him around. "You can't go in there, Hamp."

"It's my fight, Ned."

"You try to go in that hotel, Hamp, and I'll have to stop you."

"I wouldn't try it if I was you, Ned," Hamp Donnelly said softly. "You and me have been friends a long time." He jerked away from Ned Crockett and started walking up the street toward the hotel. Everyone was talking. He heard them as if from a distance. . . .

"Boyd Novis hired Tuna as a gun guard."

"Tremaine got drunk last night and lost a lot of money."

"The game was crooked."

"We ought to hang Stinson and run Novis out of town."

"Hamp!" Ellen's voice was clear and strong, close to his elbow. She reached out and tried to stop him. "Hamp," Ellen said. "I can't stand any more of it." He kept walking. "Hamp!" She was crying now. "It doesn't matter, Hamp. Nothing matters. Let Novis have Anchor. Let them have what they want. It isn't worth your life—" Her voice faded behind him, a broken sob that stayed with him and was with him when he entered the deserted lobby of the hotel.

He drew his gun and crossed the lobby

to the foot of the stairs, keeping to one side. "Tuna?" His voice echoed through the empty building.

"Up here, Donnelly." Tuna's voice was heavy, taunting. "Come on up and have a drink."

"Stay away from here, Donnelly!" Boyd Novis was with Tuna. The sheepman's voice was charged with fear.

There was a potted fern on the newel post. Hamp reached out and pushed it over. It hit the floor with a crash and the pot broke. Two shots cracked out in rapid succession, and splinters jumped from the floor at the foot of the stairs. The balled plant rolled back and forth on the floor. There was a long silence. "How about that, Donnelly?" Tuna called.

"High and to the left," Hamp yelled. "You'll have to do better than that." He picked up a bentwood chair and threw it against the lobby desk. Tuna didn't fall for the trap.

Carefully, then, Hamp edged his way along the wall, into the dining room and out into the kitchen. He thought of the outside covered stairway that led to the second floor. Ned Crockett would have guards posted there. Hamp decided he would have to risk it. Snatching up a dish towel, he opened the back door and waved the towel and then dashed out. He heard a voice say, "There he goes!" A rifle bullet tore into the wooden wall, and Hamp was around the corner and into the protection of the covered stairway.

He stood there, panting, and then he started up, a step at a time, testing each board with his feet. He opened the door of the second floor, his gun in his hand, and he was in the far end of the dark hallway. Boyd Novis's room was down toward the front window.

It seemed like an hour that he waited. Then the door of Novis's room inched open. It opened out, and it was between Hamp and the man who was opening it. Tuna's voice was loud. "You still down there, Donnelly?"

"Right here, Tuna."

There was a burst of gunfire, and the panel of the door splintered outward. Tuna was firing through the door, hiding behind it. Hamp threw himself across the hall and now he could see Tuna behind the door. He fired once, saw Tuna turn. He could see that battered face, the stringy hair hanging from under the black hat. He remembered Orvie

Stinson and how Orvie had looked falling down that covered stairway. . . . A bullet tore a furrow in the wall at the side of Hamp's head, and now he was firing back, the gun bucking against the palm of his hand. He saw Tuna crash back against the doorjamb, saw him try to raise the gun. Tuna's hand opened. The gun dropped and Tuna slid down the doorjamb. He sat there on the floor a full second before he fell to one side.

Hamp Donnelly walked down the hall, the gun still in his hand. He turned in at the door, and Boyd Novis was crouched behind his desk. "Don't come in here, Donnelly. I warn you!"

Hamp holstered his gun and walked into the room.

"I didn't have anything to do with this, Donnelly," Novis squealed. "This was a fight between you and Tuna Stinson. Everybody knows that!"

"You've got an IOU against Paul Tremaine?" Hamp asked.

"And I'll collect it, too! It had nothing to do with this. Tremaine was a crazy drunk. He tried to kill me—"

"Let me have that IOU."

"You stay away from me! You haven't got any right to that!" Novis was standing now, a withered little man, too small for his clothes, a man who had hated his size all his life. Paul Tremaine's IOU was there on the desk. Hamp picked up the piece of paper and Novis screamed at him. "I'll have the law on you! That IOU is perfectly legal!"

Hamp moved around the desk and Novis backed away, his eyes wide. He kept watching the piece of paper in Hamp's hand, saw Hamp work it into a ball. "I'll collect it, I tell you," Novis said weakly.

Hamp thrust the balled paper in front of Novis's face. "Eat it," Hamp said. His left hand shot up and he gripped Novis's cheeks between thumb and forefinger and squeezed the way he might have opened the mouth of a stubborn horse. "Eat it and swallow it, sheepherder," Hamp said.

Boyd Novis stood there, panting and choking, gagging on the mangled paper. "I'll get you, Donnelly," he raved. "I'll drive you out of the country. I'll buy Anchor and every other piece of land around here and I'll drive you out of the country!"

"You're whipped, Novis," Hamp said quietly. "You're whipped all the way." He stood there looking at Novis, and gradually his anger died, leaving only disgust. "You might as well get used to it, Novis," Hamp said softly. "If you owned every acre of land in Oregon it wouldn't make you two inches taller."

Hamp turned and walked out into the hall and down the stairs and out onto the street. There was a silent crowd around the entrance to the hotel.

He saw the marshal and he nodded, indicating that it was over. "Sorry I had to cross you, Ned," he said.

The marshal looked at him; his eyes were hard, but there was understanding in them. "I could have stopped you if I had wanted to, Hamp," he said.

Hamp Donnelly looked at the man he had known a long time, a young man, good-looking, capable. He thought of Sue. "I believe you could have, Ned," he said. He walked on through the crowd and he saw Sue and Ellen. Sue had her arm around Ellen's waist. Hamp stood by them, but they didn't see him. . . .

"I didn't know about you and Dallas, Sue," Ellen said. "I didn't know anything about it."

"It's all right, Ellen," Sue Donnelly said. "I've been trying to learn to hate him for a long time. Now that it's happened I'm surprised at how very easy it is."

Hamp walked over and put his arm around Ellen's shoulder. "I'll take you home," he said. "Your friends here will take care of things."

Dallas Rombeck watched them drive out of town. He knew it was over here for him, just as it had been over in The Dalles and in Portland. And what had until this moment been terror turned into a consuming rage against Hamp Donnelly. He saw Ned Crockett and he ran up to him and gripped the lapels of Ned's coat. "Are you going to let him drive off like that? Don't you know anything about the law you are supposed to enforce? He killed a man, didn't he?"

Ned Crockett reached up and unpinned the badge from his shirt and dropped it into his pocket. He unbuckled his gun belt and then let it drop to the ground. He looked at Sue Donnelly, and she met his eyes. She was a little bewildered, a bit contrite. . . . "Sure, Dallas," Ned Crockett said. "I'm gonna do something." His fist traveled six inches, and Dallas went over backward, his hands shoulder-high. Ned Crockett reached down and got his gun belt and fastened it around his middle. He took the star from his pocket and pinned it back on his shirt. "I'm sorry, Sue," he said. "It's just that I been wantin' to do that for a long time."

She met his eyes, soft and understanding. "It's a wonder you didn't want to hit me," she said.

The shadows were blue across the rolling hills above Antelope. There was sun only on top of the butte. There were a thousand things Hamp Donnelly wanted to say, but now he felt there would be a thousand nights in which to say them. Most of all he wanted to tell Ellen that he still wanted her to stay and that he wanted her to stay here forever. Ahead of them, on the road toward Anchor, three buggies left a trail of dust.

"I wonder who that is?" Ellen said. Her voice was dead and empty.

"Neighbors," Hamp said. "Folks from town. They'll be coming out to stay with you and help any way they can—" He heard her quick sob.

They stopped at the summit, and the wind was fresh off the sage and it flattened the dry grass in silver patches. The butte seemed near in the gathering evening, and the sun built a bonfire on the table top. He put his arm around her and held her close so that she could see the butte, but he didn't look at her face. He was looking off across the land, a land he understood, a land that he wanted her to know.

"I think Dusty would like it if Paul were buried up there beside him," Hamp said quietly.

She clutched his shirt and hid her face against his chest. "Paul—"

"He acted like a man, Ellen," Hamp said. His lips were against her hair, so lightly that she didn't know. "No one can do more than that."

The evening gathered into dusk, and the purples and golds came down out of the hills and faded into the blue of the canyons. It was over now. She had to realize that. All the nights she had waited up for Paul—all the love and understanding she had tried to give him. It had all led to this day. . . .

She turned and looked once at the butte and then she was gazing out into the gathering shadows. The hills were soft and blue and permanent and they would be there forever. Yes, she decided, this was Paul's place. And it was her place, too, for once Paul was buried here he would be a part of this and she would be a part of it. A part of herself would be buried with Paul. . . .

"I hired a hay crew," Hamp said. "I'll have them hold off a week or so."

She thought of Anchor and of what it had meant to her uncle and to Hamp, and she wondered if someday it would mean the same to her. It had to mean as much, because now she knew she would stay here always. She felt Hamp's arm strong around her. "No," she said. "Don't hold the crew up. We'll have to get our hay in before it rains."

He looked at her and was proud of her, and she thought of how much he was like the land, a strong land, even cruel at times, but a permanent land, a thing to cling to. She raised her lips to his and the world was their own. Yes, she thought, Hamp Donnelly was like the land. And a woman could learn to love the land and give herself to it completely. She knew now that that was so.